Strangers Move On

It was mid-summer in Colorado when gunfighter Clay Bodie rode into town with the sunrise, searching for peace.

But wild Big Bend was not a peaceful town – until Bodie chose to stay on and make it so – no matter what it cost in gunsmoke. . . .

Strangers Move On

Ryan Bodie

A Black Horse Western

ROBERT HALE · LONDON

© Ryan Bodie 2010
First published in Great Britain 2011

ISBN 978-0-7090-9079-3

Robert Hale Limited
Clerkenwell House
Clerkenwell Green
London EC1R 0HT

www.halebooks.com

Typeset by
Derek Doyle & Associates, Shaw Heath
Printed and bound in Great Britain by
CPI Antony Rowe, Chippenham and Eastbourne

CHAPTER 1

MAN ALONE

It was midsummer in Colorado and the land was red and brown where the man rode, with small patches of green showing only beneath the trees and the rocky overhangs. The last rainstorms had fled months earlier into the north and the little rivulets cut in the scarred earth were now filled with dust and dead seed. With dark eyes that looked as if they had seen too much, the horseman could note that this was anything but prosperous country. Those few who called this remote valley home would scratch hard for a living from the grudging earth and the rewards would always be poor, he speculated.

The wind was uncertain as it always was just before dawn. It fingered the dark pines that clothed the upper reaches of Bear Claw Pass and drove away the thin clouds. The morning light was no more than a grey bar along the rimrock which slowly spread upwards into the east, banishing the last of the night's darkness, the slow clip-clop of hoofbeats echoing from the walls of the pass.

The rider grimaced, feeling no pity for the farmers and ranchers who called this region home. For there were far worse ways of making a living than working this hard scrabble earth. There was his way.

That heavy mood was still with him, he realized. Always, following a gunfight, Clay Bodie felt this way, yet the depression had never lasted this long before. It was three weeks now since Aaron Platte had sought him out in the Devilrider Saloon in Toryville, three long weeks since that gunman had gone down beneath a thunderclap of Colts without even getting his six-shooters clear of leather.

Yet still Bodie rode on, driven to search for peace . . . or maybe something as simple as anonymity.

Maybe at last he would find it here in Toryville, he mused, and wondered cynically whether he even halfway believed that.

He shut out the thoughts and rode on through the glory of a Colorado sunrise and into the morning, the day already hot with the sun still only an hour above the horizon.

His way led past a sagging frame shack that stood well back from the trail.

Around the building straggled a rusted wire fence

with tumbleweeds piled against it here and there and many of the posts leaning over as if they also were weary of heat and dust.

A woman, dark-faced and slatternly, filled the doorway of the building and stared out at him with dull eyes. A tow-headed boy appeared from behind the rusted hulk of a capsized water tank, watching his approach without expression.

No doubt, he mused, somewhere up in back of the house there would be a worn-out man wrestling with a plough that had collapsed for the dozenth time that day against the unyielding claypan.

Bodie had passed by many such places that week. Some day, long after all spirit had been drained from overworked bodies by the brutal life, they would surrender and leave. But until that day they would struggle and fight against impossible odds. And in a way he envied them.

The boy stared at him with deep-blue eyes as he reined in at the title gate. The kid's eyes were his best feature. He was plain as a snubbing post, yet he was still somebody's son. He would surely live longer than a gunslinger's only legacy, his notorious name.

Bodie drew a coin from his pocket and turned the shiny double eagle between thumb and forefinger.

'How far to the next town, kid?'

The boy's eyes were fixed on the coin. 'Five miles as the crow flies.'

'How far as a horse walks?'

'Ten.'

'What's the place called?'

'Big Bend.'

Big Bend. Bodie nodded in approval. He liked the sound of that place – mainly because he'd never heard of it. And maybe, by some miracle, Big Bend had never heard of Clay Bodie.

'Obliged,' he grunted. He flipped the coin in a glittering arc and the kid snatched it with the sureness of a trout taking a fat fly.

The boy said nothing, just stared down at the coin in his palm. It would likely have to keep him and his ragged-ass family for a week or maybe two, the gunman mused as he rode on – yet he still half-envied them.

He travelled several miles before sighting smoke smudging the landscape ahead, indicating a town. He guided his big sorrel beneath a scrawny cottonwood out of the sun and swung down.

He ground-tied the mount then watered it sparingly from his camp-skillet after removing the heavy Texas saddle, before hunkering down to make a light meal out of jerked beef and cornpone.

There was the same economy of motion in the way he ate as the way he did everything else. He was a young man with old eyes dressed in a black leather shirt and Levis. Chest and shoulders were solid, tapering down to lean hips and legs. Black hair was worn shoulder-length and a neat moustache lined his upper lip. When he drew out the mother-of-pearl case from his pocket to select a Red Man cigar, his actions were as deliberate as if he were lining up a killer in his gunsights.

A horseman appeared along the dusty trail when he was halfway through his cigar. The man proved to be a barbed-wire salesman on his way to Big Bend, and though obviously keen to reach his destination and wrap his fist round a cold beer, he delayed and made small talk while studying the seated stranger closely.

Suddenly he broke off talking, and Bodie could almost see his brain working.

'By glory, I knew I'd seen your face before, stranger!' he exclaimed. 'You're that pilgrim the papers are always writin' up, ain't you? Clay Bodie, the gunslinger – right?'

Bodie made no response. He just stared up at the man with such intensity that the salesman first grew uncomfortable, then began to fidget. He finally excused himself with a nervous mutter and rode off much faster than when he'd arrived.

The gunfighter didn't stir before the horseman disappeared in the direction of the distant town. Then he rose with the dead cigar jutting out from beneath his moustache and his eyes were bitter. What a fool he'd been to believe this place might be different from any other. He'd been recognized and knew he could be dead certain that pot-bellied drummer would make sure he alerted Big Bend about who on his way in.

Saddling up again, he stared off at the towering, snow-covered peaks of the Snow Wolf Mountains far to the south. They beckoned, yet he resisted. He'd been on the high lonesome three weeks now. He'd had a bellyful of being alone. He nursed a slender hope that Big Bend might prove to be the kind of place where they wouldn't hold a man's reputation against him even if they did figure out just who and what he was.

Half an hour's ride brought the town into sight. He reined in sharply, showing surprise. The town wasn't big but looked solid and prosperous where it sprawled out from the base of a hill that was dominated by a splendid mansion of timber and stone.

Poor country, yet a prosperous looking town – surely an odd combination? He was envisioning a good hotel bed, well-cooked meals and maybe a pretty girl of some style to pour him a blended bourbon, as he rode on in.

Dalton, the storekeeper, sighted him first as he rode into Abraham Street, but immediately decided he didn't look like customer material and went on picking his teeth.

Haines Hall of the Big Bend Stage and Freight Company, felt an uneasy twinge in his well-filled stomach as the lone rider plodded past, while Forgen the hotelkeeper squinted from his doorway and was

10

surprised. His impression of the stranger was that of a cold-eyed hellion who could put the chill of the grave on a man from a hundred yards off. He reckoned this dark-garbed young stranger looked almost a gentleman despite the .45 riding low on his right thigh.

From the window of his law office, Sheriff Sadler watched and rubbed the side of his big nose, a sure indication that Big Bend's peace officer felt suddenly nervous. Directly across at the Tambourine Saloon, Mayor Burney reassured his drinking buddies that should this gunpacker cause trouble then the general would certainly take care of him. Somehow the general always managed to handle things just right.

At the other end of all this inspection, Bodie was assessing the town with deepening interest. There wasn't a boarded-up business or one unpainted building to be sighted the whole length of Main.

He stroked his jaw and studied the hotel while wondering what held this town together. This wasn't farming country, while Big Bend didn't have the look of a mining community. And judging by the poor standard of the stock and scrawny cattle he'd passed on the way in, it wouldn't rate as any kind of cow town. Seemed this was a place that existed for no particular reason yet was obviously doing well.

Mighty curious.

The Wagon Wheel was smaller than the

Tambourine but also reflected the town's prosperous character. The backboard was made of mahogany, and when the newcomer sauntered in and ordered his favourite Old Atlanta bourbon, he got just what he asked for.

He stood sipping and looking the place over.

A smooth bartender. A gentleman drunk in a far corner asleep in his chair. Four men playing stud at another table, a faded saloon angel in gaudy finery leaning against the bar with a cigarette angling from the red wound of her mouth.

He looked straight ahead at the bar mirror as he sipped his whiskey, but knew they were watching him. He was accustomed to that, knew strangers had trouble trying to figure what brand he wore. He looked something like a gunslinger, yet somehow non-threatening – or so he'd been told. He might have been a simple cowhand with an expensive Colt .45 riding his hip. Didn't look aggressive, and yet by the same token, strangers were rarely tempted to strike up a conversation.

The whiskey was just fine; Old Atlanta always was. He sometimes seriously doubted he would have reached his current twenty-five years of age without the Red Man Cigars and Old Atlanta whiskey.

'So, passin' through, stranger?' the balding barkeep managed to get out after a time.

They always asked that after eventually figuring out the brand he wore, he mused.

12

'Could be, or maybe not,' he replied. Then, with more emphasis, 'But reckon I'll be around a spell, I guess.' And knew just how weary he was of running.

Toting hat and glass to a far corner he sat facing the room and lit up a Red Man cigar. Smoke curled around his lean and handsome features as he leaned back in the chair and crossed one boot over the other. Through the open window he could see a strip of the main stem. A butcher in a striped apron stood out front of his shop, rocking on his heels. No sign of a customer, yet his window was well stocked, the shop itself obviously built to last.

The gunfighter smiled to himself. Why was he so curious about so many signs of affluence in such an everyday kind of town? Maybe these folk had simply learned the big secret of doing well without working your insides out all day long?

Barely had that possibility registered with him when the rear door of the saloon crashed open and a booming voice filled the room.

'*Bodie!*'

He stiffened.

How often had he heard his named called, just like that? He saw that the man who'd come busting in was around his own age, lean and likely-looking and sporting a heavy gunbelt. Bodie had never sighted him before, he knew instantly.

The stranger stabbed a finger at him.

'You are Bodie, the bloody-handed gunslinger!'

13

The sigh he exhaled at this was tinged with weariness, the implication of that truculent challenge only too familiar. When a man wore a Colt tied down, his rep always arrived ahead of him; there was a certain breed of small-town trouble-maker who just had to start up something, when all a man craved was a quiet corner, a soothing shot of bourbon, a little peace.

There was a pattern to such situations, he thought bitterly, and it rarely varied. He'd genuinely hoped this town might prove different, but he only had to meet that hopped-up stare and the cocky stance of the fool with the gun to know it was just like Cole City, Donnybrook, Mesa Grove.

He sensed it wouldn't work, yet he tried the silent treatment, hefting his glass, taking a sip, staring vacantly off at the batwings.

'Hey! Look at me – woman-killer!'

He turned his head, set the glass to one side. Would he have to kill another man before he could pick it up again?

'What do you want, sonny?' his voice was cold.

'Your name's Bodie, right?'

'You know it.'

'And you are the gunfighter?'

'Yeah.'

'Then get to your feet on account I'm gonna cut you down!'

The idiot didn't really look the type, he realized as

14

he studied him. No flashy gunslinger breed, but rather heavily built and sunburned like a working-man. He didn't have that vain, half-wild look about him that usually marked the glory-hunting amateur bent on bracing Clay Bodie simply because he stood so tall.

He flicked a glance at the bar where the girl and the barkeep stood staring. He thought both appeared astonished, as if maybe they were finding this big-mouth's actions out of character.

'Has this fool got any friends in this dump?' he asked loudly. 'If so, then get him the hell out of here before he makes me kill him.'

'I said get to your feet!' the man raged, hand hovering over gun handle. 'I'm goin' to kill you for what you done to my sister!'

A nerve began to twitch in Bodie's cheek. That line was also familiar. When would-be gunners had no reason on God's earth to kick up a gunfight, they would often dream up a wronged sister, mother or travelling salesman to justify their actions and pump up their bogus rage.

And yet this man still didn't look like that all-too familiar breed somehow. He looked like an everyday citizen driven by a genuine rage.

How come?

Bodie rose, displaying the smooth economy of action that marked everything he did.

'What's your name?'

'Blayney West. You killed my sister in Dodge City three months back.'

'I haven't been to Dodge in a year. And I've never shot a woman.'

'She was in the crowd when you shot it out with Chot Tyler. She was cut down by a stray shot from your gun. She was all the kin I had in the world, Bodie . . . so go for your iron, you woman-butcherin' bastard!'

'What good will it do your sister if you get killed too?' he growled, wondering if maybe the idiot might be telling the truth.

'That's sure somethin' to ponder on, Blayney!' The barkeep called from the rear. 'And what about your wife, man?'

'Shut up!' West snarled. 'Look, Bodie, I know you done it, so go for your iron or so help me I'll cut you down where you stand!'

Bodie made no move.

'Draw, you crawlin' snake!'

He didn't know how long the taunting might continue. Sometimes you could string it out long enough for the rube, hick or would-be gun king to get cold feet and quit. He was prepared to wait until Blayney West's hand went for his gun before he would make a move. Then he would have to kill him.

All colour drained from West's face, and this too was characteristic of this breed. Soon the mouth would firm, the eyes narrow, then he would grab for

16

that big, clumsy-looking Colt, sagging lop-eared from his gunbelt.

And for just the shaved tip of a second, Bodie, the fast gun, found himself musing, why not let the hick come clear and start blasting? Let it end here before he found himself forced to kill some hick who you could bet was slower than a fly in molasses? Mightn't that be better than spending the rest of your life waiting for the next hick bent on suicide to brace you?

Next moment it happened, when West's eyes glittered crazily and he made a frantic grab for gun handle.

Bodie's hand blurred instantly, driven by reflexes that never failed or even slowed. Now the weapon was in his hand, was sweeping upwards while his opponent was still jerking and grimacing to get that old weapon clear of leather, his eyes crazy with rage, his skill and gunspeed pathetic to watch.

Surely even a hate-crazed idiot could see he didn't have the hope of a snowball in hell?

But Blayney West was an angry fool, and not even the chilling sight of the gunfighter's gleaming Colt trained on his chest could could stop him finally levelling the weapon on his adversary, eyes wild with murderous intent.

'Then die!' Bodie raged, and his finger jerked hard on trigger.

The buck of his Colt against his hand was as familiar as the pungent whiff of gunpowder. West grunted as deep as his liver as the slug smashed into his thick body. His expression was one of surprise and shock. All the anger was gone in a moment, and now came the terror.

West staggered backwards against the bar, bending slowly forwards as though ill. His thick arms clasped his belly, but Bodie knew the pain was centred higher, at heart level.

Then West slowly slumped to the floor and lay there curled up, never to move again.

The old feeling engulfed Bodie, the familiar pang of bitter regret over something which he'd had to do which could never be undone. He gazed beyond the frightened faces and heard the shouting in the street and felt he wanted to run yet knew he could not, would not. He was too proud to run, too deathly tired.

Turning his back on the dead man, he returned to his table to wait for the law. He drained his half-filled glass. The liquor was like acid against his teeth.

Spiders had spun their delicate webs across the windows and the afternoon sunlight filtered through. The tumbledown shack at the end of Lee Street wasn't much, but was home to Manny Martin, the town drunk.

Manny had been vaguely surprised upon his return from Abraham Street with a jug of cheap wine to find a stranger occupying his battered front porch, but quickly relaxed, glad of the company.

Most of Big Bend might be feeling fearful of the dark-headed young gunfighter right at that moment, yet the only genuine fear ragged Manny ever experienced was that the day might come when they would stop tramping plump grapes to make red wine.

Bodie had sought out the dump deliberately – not quite out of town but far enough removed from Main Street to satisfy a man in need of solitude. He'd thought the place abandoned, but when the ragged occupant showed up he didn't care. Manny was gabby in drink and almost amusingly entertaining.

The booze-hound painted a picture of life in Big Bend while his 'guest' smoked a cheroot and brooded on the shooting.

The sheriff who'd questioned him was plainly a good, honest peace officer, yet like most others here was firmly in the general's hip pocket.

Gabby Manny had told him all about General Richter, the town's pre-eminent citizen and owner of the great mansion on the rise above the town.

Manny freely admitted that he and the general represented the social extremes in town. The general owned half the town and was said to be filthy rich. A bachelor who employed a staff of twenty, the man was reputedly a Civil War hero with apparently unlimited powers here in town. He warned a poker-faced Bodie that his gunning a citizen down might well be viewed

19

unkindly by the general, in which case it might be wise for him to saddle up and hightail, if he got his meaning.

Bodie just grunted. He had no solid reason for staying on here, but his gunfighter's pride would never permit himself to be moved on or intimidated. So he was still there at the shack, sipping raw whiskey and yarning desultorily when they sighted the sheriff heading off up Richter Hill.

'Looks a heap like he's headin' up to the big house to put all the facts before the general,' Manny Martin remarked. He looked pointedly at the gun-fighter as if expecting him to saddle up and head for the tall and uncut if he knew what was good for him.

But he didn't.

CHAPTER 2

STRANGERS MOVE ON

Afternoon sunlight slanted silently through the even rows of pines that clothed the slopes of Richter Hill as Sheriff Milt Sadler rode up towards the general's mansion.

The citizens of Big Bend regarded the Richter house with great pride even though it wasn't part of the town itself. The building stood with imposing grandeur on the crest of a timbered hillside slope on the high southern side of the town. It was constructed in the Gothic style and was built to last, just like the great mansions of the rich in the Eastern States on which it had been patterned.

The whole place had an air of permanency, which was the way the general liked it. On arriving at this corner of Colorado three years earlier, Richter had immediately set his roots down deep. He liked to proclaim that even if called by the people to represent them in the Senate Chamber in the East one day, Big Bend would always remain his home and his great mansion would always be there for him to return to and to remind folks that he was still very much the power in the land.

He liked to think that in a hundred years' time, when he was dead and gone, local folks would still point his place out to visitors and say, 'That there is the Richter mansion.'

The sheriff never felt at ease in the great house, for Big Bend's peace officer was a man of humble origins. Nonetheless, he was obliged to visit frequently, for the general had to be kept abreast of all matters that took place in the town itself, and the lawman invariably consulted with the great man whenever anything blew up.

Such as that morning's shoot-out at the Wagon Wheel Saloon, for example.

The sheriff knew better than ever to reach a major decision without the general's full knowledge and approval. As a consequence he was at that moment informing the big man about one Clay Bodie and how come Blayney West happened to be lying stiff and stark in Jackson's Funeral Parlour even as they spoke.

The general listened in silence, then nodded briskly.

'Plainly this Bodie is bad medicine. Kick him out of town and see he stays gone.'

The gunfighter didn't prove hard to find and the lawman located him easily where he stood relaxed in afternoon shadows smoking a cigarette and absently watching a pair of silk-stockinged legs go switching by.

The lawman cleared his throat and ran a bony finger round his shirt collar as his mount carried him closer to the saloon. Sadler was a good, reliable town sheriff who would most likely get himself re-elected year after year even without the general's backing, yet he wasn't much of a hand at managing men of the fast-gun breed. Nonetheless, he knew his duty and meant to carry it out.

To the casual passer-by, Bodie appeared reasonably harmless as he stood lounging with his muscular back leaning against the saloon wall and with thumbs hooked in the heavy leather gunbelt buckled around slender hips. But the lawman was more observant than most, and instinct warned that it might well prove difficult to move this gun-toter – should he decide he didn't want to go.

Which was why he decided the only way to handle this was act tough, go in hard, get it done.

So he cleared his throat and said officiously, 'All right, Bodie, time to ride.'

'That's Mr Bodie.'

'Huh? I mean . . . what did you say?'

'You heard.'

The lawman swallowed then glanced down at his star and found the required courage.

'I ordered you to get moving, mister. So move.'

Bodie yawned and the lawman flushed.

'I gave you an order, gunman. Either mount up or I'll have to arrest you.'

'What for? For defending myself?'

'You killed a man. I don't plan to see you kill any more in my town.'

'So . . . you are posting me out of Big Bend? Is that it?'

'Posting can be a cantankerous word, gunfighter. I'd rather call it a request that you move on.'

A shadow crossed the gunfighter's face. It was the old familiar scene, he brooded. He rarely stopped over in any town without it eventually coming to this. Even if he didn't burn powder, sooner or later he would find himself confronted either by a lawman, a posse, or just a rabble of scared towners wanting him to move on. And mostly he shrugged and forked leather. Mostly. But not always. Right at that moment he had no yearning for the lonesome trails, solitary campfires . . . the drifting on until he came to a town most likely exactly the same as Big Bend. . . .

'Sorry, can't help you, Sheriff.'

'Huh?'

24

'You heard.'

'But why would you want to stay?'

'Maybe I like it here.'

Sadler felt his mouth turn dry, but he didn't quit. He was thinking of General Richter as he made his response, 'Don't go begging for trouble, young feller—'

'Who put you up to this, lawman? I'll take one guess. It was the general.' His eyes narrowed. 'I saw you riding up to that big house. Five will get you ten you got your instructions up there regarding me. You want to say that isn't so?'

The lawman ignored the query.

'The general is the most important man in the whole county,' he said stiffly. 'And what he says goes.'

Bodie nodded slowly as though this was exactly as he had it figured. Gunfighters never left folks unaffected. Some they scared, others they offended, still others took one look and started mustering support to have you moved on. Times he complied, other times he dug in the boot-heels. He could feel obstinacy rising now . . . until he glanced around to realize that a small bunch of citizens had assembled in back of him during his pow-wow with the law. They were trying to look tough but he could see plain as day they were shaking in their boots. Mr Big was most likely behind this, he guessed. Richter. He was the power here, not the badgeman. It would be Richter who wanted him gone.

He didn't speak or move for a full minute, by which time both the badgeman and his back-up party were showing signs of the cold sweats. At last he just sighed, flicked his cigar away and swung up. Visibly relieved, the sheriff indicated the north trail and they rode off together with the eyes of all Big Bend following them.

It was a familiar scene for the onlookers, for the sheriff never tolerated saddle bums, drifters or gun-fighters to clutter up his neat streets for too long. In hobo jungles and rough camps along the trails, this was known as a town to steer clear of, for most. But Clay Bodie hadn't known that and it would have made no difference if he had.

'So, where do you hail from, Mr Bodie?' Sadler asked as the last of the houses fell behind them. The man was genuinely curious. There was something about this stranger that seemed to set him apart from other gunslingers he'd encountered.

'All over.'

'No hometown?'

'San Antonio, I guess.'

'Reckoned I caught a touch of Texas in your voice. Been long gone from San Antonio?'

'Long gone. . . .'

'Can't go back?'

'Why do you ask that?'

'Well, it's most always that way with men of your stripe, isn't it? You can never go back . . . for one

26

reason or another.'

'What is my kind?'

'The gun-packing kind, of course. Shooters.'

'Maybe we don't have much choice, badgepacker. Every place we go, there's some fool or another wanting to brace our breed. You know that West fronted me and forced me to gunfight. If you didn't believe that you'd have me in the calaboose right now.'

'West was a solid citizen.'

'He was a fool. But while we're on him, badge-toter, have you got any notion where he got the loco idea that I might have killed his sister?'

'He seemed pretty sure about that.'

'I've never shot a woman and never would.' Bodie was thoughtful for a moment before deliberately adding, 'But I've put paid to a badge-toter or two in my day.'

This wasn't true. But the gunfighter was angry now and ready to lash out. The way he saw it, he'd ridden into a peaceful-looking town, had a quiet drink, then was braced by a total stranger who'd forced him to gun him down or die. He'd feigned indifference following the shootout – that was always the best defence. But this was different. For some reason he wanted this lawman to believe him.

But the sheriff made no response. The man's hands were not quite steady and he was quite conscious of how desperate this situation might become should this hard man of the gun turn on him. Sadler had seen enough of the general's bodyguard, Reb Quent, to understand the vast difference between the professional gunslinger and men like himself. He'd geared up the nerve to guide this man from his town, but his nerve had suddenly deserted him. All he wanted now was to see Bodie's back.

The shadows lengthened as they climbed. Sunset wasn't far off now. Already a welcome and cooling wind was gusting down from the crests of the Snow Wolf Mountains which were being transformed into pillars of fire by the dying sun.

They reached the high crest of the trail and reined in.

Sadler glanced sideways at the sober figure beside him. 'No hard feelin's, Mr Bodie?'

No response. Bodie was watching the sunset.

'Anythin' I can do for you?' Sadler asked. Bodie had no way of knowing that this concern was quite uncharacteristic of the badge-toter, didn't realize that in that moment the lawman was feeling something close to sympathy for him. All he felt in that moment was cold anger in his guts.

Another town. Another gunfight. Another dead man.

'I only want one thing from you, lawman.'

'What's that?'

'To be left alone. Like now!'

Sadler lifted a hand as though to speak, but

28

changed his mind and rode off without another word. Bodie took out a cigar and smoked it through as the sun plummeted from sight and the quick, cool dusk spread over the land. He finally flipped the dead butt away and with the cooling night breeze stirring his moustache, turned and started back towards the distant lights of Big Bend.

It had happened at long last.

Clay Bodie, lonely man of the gun, had finally been moved on once too often.

CHAPTER 3

THE DEEP SIX

'Cowards die many times before their deaths but the valiant taste death but once!' boomed Mayor 'Shakespeare' Burney at the funeral in town the following morning.

He paused to make sure the mourners were with him. They plainly were, so he inflated his bulky chest and continued with his eulogy.

'So it was with our noble friend and brother, Blayney West. Kind, gentle, hard-working and devoted, Brother Blayney has been reduced to the dust from which he first sprang. . . .' A pause for a dramatic sweeping gesture at the cheap casket. 'Now he lies most foully slain by one unfit to buckle his boot straps. This is a black day for us all, in the presence of outrage and tyranny!'

Heads nodded in sober agreement all around. They selected Burney as mayor year after year for two reasons. With his flowing locks and dignified manner, Burney looked the way an orator should, and added to that nobody could spill out the ten-dollar words as smoothly as he did. It did not matter that the mayor frequently mixed up his poetry with his prayers, he had the silver tongue and be it baptisms, funerals or council meetings, 'Shakespeare' Burney could always get up and make the rafters ring and give the folks what they felt was their money's-worth.

Today, half the mayor's emotion stemmed from regret for West and sympathy for his widow, the other half for immediate fear of the future. For to the shock of everybody, Blayney West's killer was back in town.

The deceased had barely a friend in the town, and the large turn-out for the ceremony was for his widowed wife. Carrie West was regarded as the most glamorous woman in the county and it was a crying shame to see her wearing widow's black at just twenty-five years of age – and her without even the comfort of a child to strengthen her in her time of grief.

The voice of the mayor drifted out over the landscape of cemetery weeds and canting headstones to carry clearly across the dusty street to reach the dark-garbed gunfighter with a crimson bandanna knotted around his throat.

The sun was now high in a vast sapphire sky beaded with puffy clouds of immaculate white. There was no hint of a breeze and the trees flanking the Abraham Street cemetery stood motionless as the mayor at last ran out of words and stepped back while men with ropes lowered the casket into the grave.

Clay Bodie was standing with arms folded in the shade of a peppercorn tree when the crowd, led by the mayor, quit the cemetery and came his way along the dusty street. The good mayor flushed, held up a hand to halt the mourners, stabbed a finger at the sky.

'An evil has come upon our fair town!' he intoned accusingly. 'Oh, that there were but one of us who had the strength and sureness of arm to smite down the one responsible for the untimely demise of our beloved brother!'

He jabbed a quivering finger at the gunfighter.

'Your time will surely come!' he bellowed, then as if alarmed by his own words, ducked his head and led the mob off down the dusty road, heading directly for the nearest bar.

The sheriff had personally escorted the gunfighter from the town last night. Yet Bodie had returned to check into the hotel, then added insult to injury by attending the burial. Some thought the sheriff should have arrested him on the spot, although when the lawman had suggested doing something about the situation he'd been unable to drum up a solitary volunteer.

With the mourners out of sight now, Bodie was about to follow when a handsome carriage flanked by outriders appeared around the Lincoln Street corner and rolled on towards the central block. Like the Richter house, the Richter coach was the finest in town, and sunlight sparkled from painted wheels and gleamed on polished harness as the rig approached the giant peppercorn tree where the single figure stood with folded arms.

As the cavalcade drew abreast of the tree, the rider travelling abreast of the coach suddenly raised a hand to bring the carriage to a halt. Through the windows could be seen a stern and vigorous looking man of around fifty, seated alongside a dark-haired woman wearing a black veil.

'That's him, Mrs West!' the man shouted. 'The murderer of your husband!'

It took a great deal to jolt the gunfighter, but that almost managed it. He'd expected the widow would have been at the graveside, wondered momentarily why she hadn't been.

His gaze played over the outriders until the leader turned his horse and reined it his way.

His right hand dropped to gun handle and his eyes were suddenly cold as sleet. Upon making his decision to return to the town where he was guilty of

nothing more than protecting himself, he'd anticipated trouble, but this was looking more threatening
than a man might have expected.

Reb Quent rode to within fifty feet of the gunfighter and reined in. Quent was ramrod of the
general's J.R. Ranch where he doubled as range boss
and bodyguard to the county's richest citizen. Lean,
intense and upright in the saddle, the rancher's
segundo radiated danger to such an extent that Bodie
flipped his cigarette aside and turned slightly to face
the horseman squarely, empty hands hanging loosely
at his sides yet very close to gunbutts.

But before a word could be spoken, the handsome
coach drew up a short distance ahead as the stern
figure leaned from a window.

'Reb!'

Just one word, yet it carried authority. In reality it
was actually the voice of a former military leader
accustomed to leadership and obedience. Reb Quent
hesitated momentarily then nodded to Bodie with a
remote expression, turned his flashy mount and
rejoined the carriage and four. For a long moment
Bodie felt the intensity of the older man's glowering
appraisal, and then abruptly the cavalcade was
moving on again.

He relaxed, not realizing he'd unconsciously
dropped into a crouch in anticipation of trouble. As
the rig rolled by he glimpsed in the rear window a
lovely oval face framed by jet-black hair staring back

at him with a look that seemed to drill into him like a bullet.

Another widow – and maybe the loveliest of them all. 'How many more might you dress in black here, Bodie?' whispered the voice of his conscience.

'There she goes!' boomed a familiar voice, and he turned his head to see the hawk-featured mayor had returned, obviously expecting some kind of confrontation. 'A saint robbed of her life's partner by a cold-blooded killer! A saint left by mindless violence. In the name of decency, why didn't you stay gone – butcher?'

Bodie's hand dropping to gun handle was an involuntary thing but its effect was instantaneous. The ashen mayor scuttled off after his party while Quent the gunman rejoined the coach which slowly started off, making for town.

Bodie grinned savagely as he stared down at the gun, then removed his hand. Had he expected to use it, he pondered. His gaze lifted to the receding coach and escort. The woman's face seemed to linger in his mind long after dust had blotted the rig from sight. She had jolted him, he realized, almost as if her censoring gaze had driven a stake of guilt clear through him that he felt he might never feel free of.

But surely that was plain loco.

He walked purposefully to where his horse was tethered, swung up and headed for the town and rye whiskey.

The back street was empty but for the rolling figure emerging from the Red Light Saloon. Back Street, Big Bend, was wide enough for Manny Martin, but not quite wide enough for him when he was toting a bellyfull of bad liquor. With total disregard for the solemn day it had been, the town's leading lush was swinging a fifth of rye in his hand and singing:

Oh, shoot 'em up, Billy,
Oh, shoot 'em up quick.
Shoot Jimmy Jackson
And his mad brother Mick. . . .

He broke off abruptly when he glimpsed the dark figure ahead on the store porch. He blinked then chuckled, took another swig, then weaved his way across.

'Why, howdy there, Bodie. What happened? Overlooked somebody you shoulda shot?'

Bodie eyed the man coldly. It must be his day to be assailed by big-mouths, he reflected. Yet considering the circumstances he reckoned it was likely no more than he might expect.

'Beat it, bum!'

Manny looked hurt. 'Hey, I thought you and me was pards, boy?'

'I don't have friends.'

36

'Join the club then, man, join the club. Here, have a shot. Double rectified busthead, guaranteed to stun a billygoat at twenty paces.'

From adjoining porches and along the plankwalk, sober citizens of Big Bend watched Clay Bodie and his staggering companion with disgust. The gunfighter, noting their disapproval, straightened his shoulders, took the bottle from Martin's grasp, wiped the neck on his sleeve and then took a drink.

They had him tabbed as a no-account killer, he mused bitterly, so he would act the part while it amused him to do so.

Then the raw spirits hit his belly causing him to wince. 'Jumped up Judas! What the hell is this?'

Manny Martin smiled fondly at his fifth. 'It's the Bottle Without a Label, Bodie boy. My daddy always warned me to steer clear of gals who wear green stockin's, and bottles with no labels. Well, I heeded that tight-fisted old polecat halfway. I quit chasin' wimmin'. Here's lookin' at you, son.'

Manny belched shatteringly, took another slug he didn't really need, then fixed the gunfighter with a curious look.

'So, what brought you back to town, Bodie ?'

Bodie was still seeing that pale face framed in the rear window of Richter's carriage in his mind's eye unbidden, and that just made him sore. Why should he feel guilty? West had given him no option but to cut him down. Even that bull jawed sheriff conceded

37

that. But then the accusing voice of conscience chimed in unbidden; 'West was so pitifully slow, Bodie . . . that's why you feel guilty!'

He shook his head impatiently.

The true reason he'd returned was the decision to quit drifting and finally make a stand some place and end the restless years of wandering.

So, he'd come back and not even the law had dared challenge his right to do so. Yet he was already beginning to look upon his decision as a mistake.

He understood why. Already his gun had sown seeds of hatred and enmity here in this lousy town, whilst the death of Blayney West was sure to attract and encourage the hot-eyed would-bes of the gun who were always suicidally ready to challenge any man with a gunslinger reputation. That idiot breed always believed that all they needed was the prospect of hanging one famous scalp on their gunbelts to elevate them to the gunfighter elite.

It was this breed which had driven Bodie from more towns than all the genuine fast guns and lawmen combined. They would surely seek him out here as they'd done in other places – he could scent it coming. And just like dumb Blayney West they would leave him with no option but to gun them down. . . .

Bodie drew a coin from his pocket, flipped it to the drunk and started off down the street. Manny bit the quarter, then slipped it away and staggered after him.

'What's the matter, pard?' he slurred. 'Don't feel like talkin', huh?'

'Right,' came the growled reply. But then curiosity got the better of the gunfighter. 'Tell me, rum-dum, how come this town looks so prosperous compared to others?'

'Why? Hell, St Judah, I guess.'

'Saint who?'

Manny Martin smiled. 'Matter of fact, this place has got two livin' saints, but I guess St Judah is number one.'

Jodie stared hard at the man. 'I guess anybody should know better than to expect a sensible answer from a lush.'

'Hell, I'm answerin' your question straight, Bodie boy. We boast two fellers here what folks treat almost like they were livin' breathin' saints. Maybe one of 'em is close enough to the real thing – namely Carrie West. Never seen a female I thought more of, and seein' just about everyone else sees her in the same light . . . well, I reckon you can understand why everybody hates your guts?'

Bodie scowled, already regretting he'd opened up. But turning his head away to spit in the dust, Manny Martin had more information to impart.

'The second livin' saint would be the general. This town was a dump dyin' on its feet when Judah Richter showed up with his big ideas and sacks of dollars and brought Big Bend back from the dead, then kept it alive ever since. Seems just about every-thin' the general touches turns to gold, and he's mighty free with his money to all kind of needy folks. Hell, some even call the old bastard St Judah, would you believe?'

'I take it you're not one of them?'

Manny shrugged and spat.

'Me and the general don't get along. That's mainly on account we don't agree on one mighty important aspect of what makes a real town, I guess. You see, I've always felt that any place like this needs a certain number of things before it rates as a real town . . . like a mayor, storekeeper, sheriff, pretty women – town drunk—'

The gunfighter almost smiled.

'Let me guess. You're the town drunk – and the general doesn't approve?'

'Got it in one.'

The gunfighter turned sober again. 'He's plenty rich, I take it?'

'Pow'ful rich.'

'How does he make his money?'

'The ranch, business interests, stock deals, I guess. At least they keep him goin'.'

'Are you saying he didn't make all his money here?'

'No sir, he was mighty flush when he got here.'

'From where?'

The drunk shrugged. 'South, so they say . . .

40

Mexico mebbe.'

Bodie was tempted to hear more about General Judah Richter, but was suddenly growing restless. Leaving a grateful Manny with a dollar bill to replenish his bottle, he went off down the street only vaguely aware that the boozer was following at a distance for a time until the pace grew too hot for him and he vanished into the next bar he passed.

Bodie kept on purposefully until he reached the livery, by which time he'd come to a decision he'd not wanted to make.

The liveryman stirred and emerged from his cubicle. 'You want your hoss, Mr Bodie?'

'Right.'

'Ain't leavin again, are you?'

'Guessed it in one.'

The liveryman's face fell. He was an individualist in a conformist town who was continually at loggerheads with the power factions. He sensed the gunfighter was a like-minded *hombre* he might get to pal up with as time went by.

'Kinda sudden decision ain't it, Mr Bodie?' he grouched as he led the horse out.

'Often they're the best kind.' The gunfighter's tone was curt. He believed he was making the right move now, even if it did come so close on the heels of his decision to give this town a genuine try-out. Plainly his vision of building something permanent in this town simply didn't stand up in the harsh light

41

of reality. Neither leopards nor gunfighters could change their spots, and a smart gunfighter recognized that fact.

The liveryman assisted him to ready for the trail, then extended a big brown hand.

'Well then, *adios*, Mr Bodie. If you ever happen by this way again. . . .'

'I won't be,' Bodie grunted, yet there was firm pressure in his handshake and a glint of friendliness in his eye. 'Steer clear of women in green stockings and bottles without a label.'

'I'll do my best, young feller,' Martin called from the doorway. 'Which way you headin' out?'

Bodie actually smiled. 'Any trail will do.' He hesitated with a frown. 'But maybe there's something I reckon I'd better do before I leave,' he added, and swung his mount away.

'He most likely aims to plug somebody else afore he goes,' sniffed the runty stablehand as horse and rider were swallowed by the night.

'You got the man wrong, boy,' Martin reproved. 'Anybody with half an eye can see that feller ain't no killer.'

'Try tellin' that to them he shot.'

'Yeah, well, fellers like that can pick up a certain name and get pushed into doin' things they can't help. Like Blayney pushed him. . . .'

Manny broke off, noticing the buckskin horse stabled in the nearby stall for the first time. 'Hey, ain't that West's horse?'

'Yeah,' affirmed Clancy. 'Picked up a stone in the hoof. I'm keepin' him here until he quits limpin'.' Crossing to the work-bench, the liveryman frowned as he bent to pick up a small blue pebble. 'I just finished prisin' this loose when you and the gunpacker came in.'

Inspecting the pebble, Martin frowned. 'Say, ain't this just like the kind of grit they spread across the driveway out at Richter Hill?'

'That's where it came from, sure enough. Scarce a week goes by when I don't have to dig some of that stuff out of J.R. hosses. I keep tellin' the general that stuff ain't any good for his horses, but you know him. He likes the flash look of it, and everyone knows how stubborn he can be.'

'Yeah, reckon so,' Manny Martin murmured. His manner was vague. He was turning the stone in his fingers and reflecting upon who may have taken Blayney West out to Richter Hill and the general before he died. For the whole county knew West and Richter had been on real bad terms for long months before that visit.

Mighty strange that . . . considering the fact that those high-rollers were two of the hardest haters in the whole county.

CHAPTER 4

'DON'T PUSH ME'

She sat alone in the quiet house, still wearing her black dress, hands lying motionless in her lap.

Somehow she had managed at last to get rid of the neighbours, the good ladies from the Big Bend Ladies' Society, and even the general.

It was now blissfully quiet in that small, white-painted house on Lee Street. The front room shades were partly closed, the faint light from the street touching familiar objects that were all a reminder of her late husband. Everything spoke of his presence which had been so swiftly and so finally taken from her.

Upon the mantlepiece stood a framed photo-graph of the happy pair on their wedding day in Texas. The local newspaper had called them the handsomest couple in the town's history. The picture depicted a dark-haired and slender girl alongside a tall, dashing-looking man with perhaps a hint of weakness in the smiling mouth. Blayney and Carrie West, joined together that day in holy wedlock until death would them part.

The young woman lifted her gaze and sighed. The general had ordered flowers for the house and the air was sickly with their overpowering scent. She should open a window, but it scarcely seemed worth the effort.

Despite her weariness and state of mind, Carrie West sat very erect upon the straight-backed chair. She had been drilled in good posture at the Academy For Young Ladies in Washington, along with all those other social graces that had once seemed to her such a waste of time.

Carrie had wed beneath herself. Her many friends back in Texas had believed this, and it was a whisper that had followed them to Big Bend, Colorado. She was the daughter of a wealthy businessman who had expected his daughter might marry into their own class, but instead she had settled for West, described as a 'handsome nobody'.

She'd always known her parents were bitterly disappointed about the marriage, but she hadn't cared. The young bride considered her husband to be handsome, dashing and exciting and was totally captivated – at first.

But gamblers make poor husbands in the main, and much of the gilt had worn off their young marriage by the time they came west to Big Bend where Blayney promptly took up the search for the Lost German Mine.

She was caring and understanding even as their situation deteriorated and her husband took to the drink, and was seldom home. Now he was dead, cut off without a warning or goodbye, hurled headlong into eternity without even a final kiss. . . .

The young woman rose suddenly and moved restlessly through the quiet house. The general's flowers were in every room, and there was a vase filled with roses in the hallway.

Richter had been very kind to her. He was a rock in a world that had turned into a nightmare.

The gate creaked and steps sounded on the flagged footway. Carrie paused in the curtained gloom of the bedroom. She could not possibly cope with any more sympathizers. If it was somebody to see her, she would not answer the door. She'd never felt more like being alone.

The soft chime of spurs carried faintly into to the room and her hand went to her throat. Knuckles sounded on the door. She didn't move.

'Mrs West?'

She frowned, not recognizing the voice. Surely no total stranger would be so unfeeling as to call on her at such a time?

46

Another knock.

'Ma'am?'

Quietly she moved into the hallway. Two narrow windows flanked the front door. She glimpsed a shoulder and arm clad in fine black leather. Another knock. She shifted again until she could clearly see the horse tied up at the gate.

It was that gunfighter's horse!

She didn't remember going to the bureau drawer and taking out the small, nickel-plated revolver her father had given her upon learning that her husband intended taking her out to the wild frontier of Colorado.

She moved like somebody sleepwalking as she raised the weapon to shoulder level using both hands to train the sights upon the door, then called:

'Come in. It's not locked!'

The handle turned and the door swung inwards. He stood outlined against the glare of the street, a man with broad shoulders and narrow hips, a man with eyes which seemed to take in everything at a single glance yet showed no fear at sight of the gun. He made no attempt to move aside, not even when she screamed, 'Murderer!'

No response from Clay Bodie. He stood with one hand still holding the door handle, his lethal right arm crooked away from his body. Their glances met and locked and it was a vividly dramatic moment in life for both the distraught young widow and the

47

man of the gun.

'I'll kill you!' Carrie West cried.

'Go ahead . . . I won't stop you.'

Her eyes widened. *This* was a killer? The breed which the general insisted should be 'hunted down like the dog he is and exterminated for the general good'.

The woman's hands had stiffened. She had to call upon all her strength to squeeze the trigger, and even as the sharp little explosion rocked the hallway she knew she had missed . . . sensed she had deliberately done so.

The gunfighter still had not moved.

A wave of unreality washed over the woman and the gun fell to the carpet with a dull thud. With her face buried in her hands, Carrie West seemed in danger of collapsing to the floor until strong arms went about her.

'Just cry it all out,' he said gently. 'It helps . . . and believe me, I should know.'

It might have been his choice of words, the reassuring tone of his voice – or simply her own physical and emotional weakness that caused the woman to lean against him for a moment as though afraid she might fall. She wanted to scream and rake at his face but all she could do was weep as though she might never stop.

It seemed a long time before the spasm ceased, and when she opened her eyes eventually she was astonished to find herself stretched full length upon the bed with her pearl-grey blanket over her. She struggled to rise but a strong hand prevented her moving further.

'You passed out,' a voice said, and she recognized who it was. 'Just take it easy while I get rid of them for you.'

She stared up at him, eyes blazing yet seemingly helpless. 'How dare you—' she flared, then paused as something he'd said registered. 'Get rid of who?' she panted. 'What—?'

'The neighbours heard the shot. I'll go tell them everything's all right.'

He quit the room immediately and it was with a feeling of unreality that the woman sat listening to the voices from the front room. At last there was silence and she realized he was now standing in the doorway with hat in his hands – the tall and impressive silhouette of the man she would hate until the day she died.

'Why did you dare come here?' she hissed. 'Have you no pity . . . or shame?'

'I just came to tell you I'm sorry.'

'Why should you be sorry? You're a killer. Your kind love to kill.'

'I sure enough don't love it, ma'am, but that makes no nevermind.' Bodie's knuckles showed white as he clutched his hat, his obvious physical tension contrasting with the quiet calm of his words.

'I'm quitting Big Bend, but before I go I just had to see you and swear to you that your husband gave me no choice but to gun him down.'

Carrie swallowed painfully. She was enraged with herself for finding him somehow convincing and sincere, when she knew that he was simply a bloody killer. Then suddenly she was stricken by a thought that immediately filled her with doubt.

'You . . . you were prepared to allow me to kill you,' she said wonderingly. 'In God's name, why?'

'There are worse things than being killed, Mrs West, There is living with yourself after killing . . . even if you had no choice. . . .'

Swinging her feet to the floor, Carrie West sat staring up at him as conflicting emotions flickered across her pale features. She was both amazed and half-ashamed that her anger seemed to be deserting her during those long moments of silence. Was she too exhausted to want to see this man dead, or was his seemingly genuine regret and exhaustion in the face of what had happened actually real and not contrived?

She searched for words as she turned away from him. 'They . . . they told me Blayney accused you of killing his sister. . . .'

'That's so, ma'am. I can understand a man getting riled about something like that. Only thing, I haven't been in Dodge City for years. I take it your husband's sister was special to him?'

There was something in his voice and manner that was soothing and calming, she realized grudgingly. She bit her lip as she considered his question. For the truth of it was that Rebecca *had* been special to Blayney. The girl had idolized her only brother, hated his wife, had financed many of his wildcat mining expeditions. Her death had been a blow from which Blayney never recovered and Carrie was hating herself now for having believed he had thought far more of her money than he'd done of his waspish sister.

'She . . . she was a good person,' she got out grudgingly. She paused, looked up at him steadily for a long minute. 'I think I almost believe you, Mr Bodie . . . about Rebecca, I mean. . . .'

He nodded, 'I thank you for that, ma'am. As for that shootout in Dodge, I recollect it was a showdown between Chot Tyler and Black Bob Watson, and they gunned one another down.'

'Again, you seem convincing.'

'Do you have any notion why your husband figured it was me?'

Carrie was framing the word 'no' with her lips when the sudden clatter of hoofbeats from outside interrupted. She jumped to her feet and ran to the windows to draw back the curtains. Several J.R. riders were visible under the street lamp and Reb Quent was already dismounting. The general's bodyguard looked menacing with a naked Colt in his hand as he

51

pushed through the yard gate.

She turned with a gasp to find the gunfighter standing at her shoulder. Bodie looked grim as he peered out.

'Trouble,' he muttered.

'I'll send them away.'

His dark brows lifted as he checked out his Colt .45. 'Why would you do that, ma'am?'

He got no further as a gunbutt slammed against the front door. 'Mrs West!' Quent hollered. 'Is that there gunpacker in there with you?'

Before the woman could respond Bodie lightly touched her on the shoulder then vanished from the room like a ghost, right hand wrapped around .45 handle.

Carrie stood with both hands pressed to her breast, expecting any moment to hear the thunder of gunfire. Instead there was only the sound of voices as Reb Quent yelled at Bodie that he had orders to take him to see the general . . . and Bodie calmly complying.

She burst through the door to confront the group. 'Wait!' she cried. 'Mr Quent, what does the general want with Bodie?'

Quent paused, staring back at her with his dead-fish eyes. 'Why, just wants to talk a few things over I reckon, Mrs West.'

Carrie wasn't reassured. She respected Judah Richter highly, yet knew he could be quite ruthless on occasions.

'Please, I would rather the man simply left town,' she said.

'Sorry, Mrs West,' said Quent, 'but the general gave his orders.'

'Don't fret, ma'am,' Bodie said quietly. 'I can handle this.'

'You talk too much, gunpacker,' growled barrel-chested Zachary Clint, giving Bodie a shove. 'Mount up and let's get movin', bucko!'

What happened next was almost too swift for the eye to follow.

Recovering his balance effortlessly, Clay Bodie turned smoothly and dropped his right shoulder as he threw a short, vicious punch to the belly. The blow travelled no more than a foot yet jack-knifed Clint as if he'd run headlong into a trip wire.

As Clint crashed to the ground, Bodie, still twisting, cleared his six-gun and employed the barrel to swipe Reb Quent's six-shooter from his grasp. The Colt spun in a glittering arc and vanished into a flower bed ten feet away. Before the weapon disappeared Bodie had holstered gun, and fitting hat to head, nodded amiably.

'See what I mean, ma'am? All right, let's go see what the general's got on his mind, cowboys.'

Carrie watched Reb Quent flinch at this. Quent was no cowboy and Clay Bodie must have known it. His manner was adding insult to offence, and she noticed that Quent's hands were trembling with anger as he hunted for his Colt amongst the flowers.

She didn't know what might happen at the great house, had no notion why the general had sent for Bodie when he had. What she did know, however, as she watched them lope off down Lee Street, was that in a matter of mere minutes a full-blooded hatred had sprung up between the dark-eyed gunfighter and sinister Reb Quent. This caused the slim girl to shudder involuntarily as she scented in this clash between two men of the gun, the graveyard stench of death.

She leaned weakly against the door frame, closing her eyes and hardening her heart. By the time Richter's men had arrived, she had felt her emotion against Bodie treacherously weakening. Now she realized how wrong she had been to feel that way. For Bodie surely was the man who had slain her husband, the only man she could ever love.

'I hope they kill him!' she breathed. And almost believed she meant it.

The general saw himself as a reasonable man.

He didn't crave to own everything, so he reassured himself. He'd accepted Bodie's account of what had transpired at Carrie West's home, and thought it commendable that the gunfighter had felt moved to express his sympathy to the young widow as he'd done. The general, in fact, was quite prepared to dismiss West's death and all related to it on condition that Clay Bodie throw his leg over that big ugly sorrel and simply ride out. The general didn't care where he went just so long as he kept riding.

Cigar-smoke drifted past Bodie's face as he sat with one leg hooked over the other in the most splendid room in this magnificent home.

The general stood before the big bluestone fire-place, a small and rigidly erect gentleman of fifty with a soldier's steely gaze and jaw like a rock.

Judah Richter was smiling, something he did but rarely in the company of lesser men.

'We are both mature men of the world, Bodie,' he said in a faintly patronizing tone. 'We both realize that townships like Big Bend and men like yourself simply don't blend well. And so I see no reason why we can't solve our little problem in the straightest, friendliest way.'

Bodie took his time replying.

The two were alone in a large room that was furnished in a simple yet impressive fashion. Reb Quent had wished to remain in what the general referred to as the 'War Room', but had been banished by his employer. This had impressed Bodie, showing that Richter was a man with steel in him.

After a time he asked, 'Did you know Blayney West well, General?'

Richter's smile faded. 'I don't see that this has any relation to our discussion, sir.'

'Maybe, or maybe not.' Bodie's stare was penetrating. 'Did you?'

'I knew the man. We weren't close.'

'I've asked this question before but I'm going to put it again. Do you know the reason he came after me like he did?'

'He plainly believed you caused his sister's death.'

'Yeah. But where would he get that notion?'

'I have no idea. But we are surely wasting time, Bodie. Your answer to my query, if you please.'

But Clay Bodie was not a man to be hurried and was a picture of assurance and relaxation as he drew appreciatively on his cigar. Richter stared flatly at him for a long moment then with an impatient grunt went to the bureau to pour another whiskey.

The War Room was General Richter's favourite part of the mansion. It smelled richly of leather and mellow oak. Above the fireplace was a pair of crossed cavalry sabres and regimental colours.

Simply to enter this room was almost to hear the distant crump of cannon and the tinny screech of the bugle summoning brave men to fight and possibly die. . . .

In the carpeted corridor outside, Reb Quent paced slowly to and fro with both hands locked behind his back. The man had been with the general ever since the war. Richter still referred to him as his aide, but all Big Bend knew that his real status was that of bodyguard. This man wouldn't relax until those oak doors opened and he saw the general safe and sound again.

At the sound of a footfall outside, Richter remarked, 'My aide is growing restless, Bodie. I must confess the same applies to me.'

Bodie rose and dropped his cigar into an ash tray fashioned from a brass shell casing.

'What if I don't agree to quit Big Bend?'

'Is this a refusal?'

'No. It's just something I'd like to know.'

'Well, in that case – I would be anything but pleased.'

Bodie moved across to the big windows to gaze down upon the town below. 'They sure think a heap of you down there, General.'

'I believe that to be so.'

'And you, in turn, think a lot of the town.'

'Yes, I do.'

'Matter of fact, I reckon you must think one *hell* of a lot of Big Bend.'

'What brings you to that conclusion, sir?'

'Why, because of the way you plainly keep it alive, of course.' Bodie turned his back to the window and stared at the man directly. 'So, tell me, General, how come a town can become so important to any man that he's prepared to pump money into it year after year and hand over fist, just to keep it alive? Seems to me I've never struck any set-up quite like that before.'

Richter's taut features turned cold.

'Bodie, you have a habit of changing the subject and avoiding the central issue. My position here in Big Bend and my relationship with the town is something I don't care to explore with you, sir.'

'So, you just want my straight yes or no. Is that it?'

'That is precisely it.'

'Then it's no.'

'I see. Would it be too much to enquire why you have reached this unfortunate decision?'

'Yeah, maybe it would be.' Bodie collected his hat. He'd been ready to quit Big Bend beforehand after having proven he would not be pushed, but now the general was overplaying his hand. He flipped his hat and caught it. 'But I'll tell you anyway.' He put a hard stare on the older man. 'I'm my own man, is why.'

The two stood trading stares.

'I'm very sorry about this,' Richter got out at length, and sounded as if he meant it. He paused, then made a dismissive gesture. 'My man Reb will show you out, sir.'

'I'm used to finding my own way,' answered the gunfighter. He went to the door, paused. 'One thing, General. Keep Quent well away from me unless you want big trouble. I smell something sick on that pilgrim, and I know how to deal with that breed.'

The general's eyes were now chips of flint. 'You have the gall to denigrate another? You – a professional man-killer? Could there be anything sicker or lower than that?'

'Just heed what I say.'

Richter had picked up a leather-covered cane. He smacked it loudly against his palm – the commanding officer dealing with a difficult situation on the front line.

'Very well, Bodie. I shall keep in mind what you said. But while we are in the business of extending warnings, permit me to reply in kind.'

'Fire away.'

'Just keep away from Mrs West.'

'Why?'

'Because I say so.'

'You'll need a better reason than that.'

A flush appeared above the general's tight collar and spread slowly over his face. He was unaccustomed to this kind of defiance, yet was no headstrong fool. He had already assessed the other as a potentially dangerous man, so managed to keep a tight rein on his temper.

'I'm not obliged to explain anything to you, gunman, but I shall in this case. Mrs West is a woman of sterling character, who now – thanks to you – finds herself all alone in the world. Not only is she under my personal protection but I hope to make her my wife after a suitable mourning period has been observed. I have no intention of permitting anybody to upset my bride-to-be, sir. Do I make myself clear?'

Bodie whistled soundlessly through his teeth.

'So that's how it is! Well, nobody can accuse you of allowing the grass to grow under your boots, General, I'll grant you that.'

'You're beginning to bore me, Bodie.'

'Well, I wouldn't want to do that.'

As he spoke, Bodie stepped to the double doors and reefed them open. Quent stood there, looking startled. Bodie brushed past the man who angrily let his fingers drop to the beautifully crafted six-shooter riding his hip.

Bodie's straight back offered a tempting target to the gunpacker as he strode off down the long corridor, but the discipline of long years' service was too deeply ingrained in the gunman for him to act impulsively upon his own initiative.

Instead he turned questioningly to his employer, standing ramrod erect in the centre of the War Room. After a long moment, a pale-faced General Richter shook his head, then beckoned his man through the arched doorway. He closed both doors on the receding figure who was fifty yards away by this.

Bodie paused and glanced back, then continued on to reach the wide, tiled gallery. Pausing in the shadowed cool, he took out another stogie and stood tapping its against the lid of the cigar tin. It was the only sound to be heard here now. It was totally quiet at the J.R. headquarters, so quiet in fact that it caused a tiny rivulet of perspiration to trickle down his neck.

He whirled swiftly. No . . . nobody in back of him. He smiled to himself. Sure, he had more than held his own with Richter, yet his own reactions here alone in the whispering night told him the little man had sure made an impression. He liked to think it took the whiff of genuine danger to make Clay Bodie sweat.

He went to his horse, mounted up smoothly then rode down the tree-lined driveway across the finely chipped bluestone gravel. The long day still wasn't done, yet during its course he'd already met two people who'd impressed him far more than expected.

They were the little-big-man whom he sensed might prove to be one of the hardest characters he'd ever encountered, and a raven-haired woman who plainly hated him, yet who, for some loco reason, he knew he badly wanted to see again.

Go figure!

Mayor Roland Burney sniffed disapprovingly as he watched the gunfighter stroll on by the law office trailing cigar smoke.

'Still here!' the man snorted. 'Still polluting our pristine air with the graveyard stench that clings to all his murderous breed. I'm sure I can't imagine what the general can be thinking of, showing him leniency!'

'Mebbe the man figures that sometimes like this

it's better just to let a rattlesnake wander off on its own accord than try and chouse it away with a big stick,' drawled Sheriff Milt Sadler.

'I still say the general made a big mistake when he didn't insist that pilgrim moved on,' Burney declared emphatically, then paused as he realized his words had drawn only silence. Most folks agreed with the sheriff every time, but this was different. He was criticizing the general, and to do this so openly in Big Bend was a rare and risky play bordering on the sinful.

His face reddening, the good mayor cleared his throat and was quick to apologize. 'Doggone, a man's mouth sometimes gets to run ahead of his brain,' he said contritely, then quickly moved on to the more interesting and far less dangerous topic which had the whole town talking that day. Namely, the persistent and spine-tingling rumour that Blayney West had secretly struck it rich before he died. Like, *real* rich.

CHAPTER 5

DESPERADOES' SUNSET

Down from the mesa lands by the old New Mexico Trail, seven travel-stained men rode into Yellow Gulch at the end of yet another blazing summer's day.

The sweating horses were heavily laden with rifles and camping gear and every man, from the hatchet-faced leader to the baby-faced kid riding drag in choking dust, wore at least one six-gun at his waist. The lean and shaggy horses looked as if they had never eaten oats or felt the caress of a curry comb.

Food dominated what conversation there was to

be heard as they travelled down the twisted, deeply-rutted track that passed for a main street in Yellow Gulch. They kept plodding onwards until at last the appetizing scents from a clapboard diner feathered the senses.

'Ham and eggs,' groaned big Barney Platte as they hitched their horses to the rack.

'Mulligan stew,' added brother Huck.

The bunch tramped inside noisily, firing orders at the startled Mexican cook like gunshots then got together to tip a drunken Cousin Jack miner out of his chair, then drew two tables together in order that they might dine together and in comfort.

The ousted miner, a bulky man who warranted his nickname of Basher Mick Dulvane, turned beet-red and flexed up impressively and aggressively as he rose – until he got a clear look at his assailants, as ugly and mean-featured a bunch of strangers as he'd ever clapped eyes on.

The man quit the dive without a word and nobody missed him. The Basher never ducked a showdown where fists or boots were the weapons of choice, but a blind man could tell this bunch was of the shooter breed who just might start blasting first and make their beg-pardons later . . . so there was a mutual decision to go seek another watering hole in this lousy town.

The newcomers bellowed for vittles, and they were fast in coming, and nobody objected to Holly Platte gusting stinking cigar smoke into their weathered faces as they ate. For one thing, they were accustomed to sleeping and eating rough. For another, objecting to just about anything Holly Platte might do could prove fatal, even to close pards – or so it was rumoured.

The outlaw boss, although feared for all his rugged power, was far from full strength that night at the tail-end of a long hard ride to elude men wearing badges who might seek to do him harm.

Indeed the outlaw pack from the Burning Hills had been riding hard and living rough ever since the night Barney Platte had toted kid brother Aaron back to camp as stiff as a plank with a .45 bullet embedded in his forehead just above eye level.

Misjudgement was the cause of Aaron Platte's violent end and the raging posse staging the manhunt for his killer had been washed away at Willigan's Ford days earlier, leaving the bunch unsupported, exhausted and bitter when finally forced to quit the Burning Hills and make for the nearest town.

Revenge was virtually forgotten as the eatery was deluged with orders for steaks, beans, hot cakes and hash browns – and keep them coming.

Joe Creek stopped eating to belch. He drew a greasy coat-sleeve across his mouth, reached for a corncob. It so happened Buck Wheeler had his beady eye on the same delicacy at the same moment. The result was predictable. A slapped wrist drew a curse followed by a splatter of hot crimson as Wheeler's iron fist slammed Creek clear out of his chair.

The pair lunged to their feet, booting over their chairs and snarling like dogs ready to tear one another apart over just one lousy piece of corn.

Holly Platte didn't join in the brawling or even the cursing and shouts of encouragement that rose to the smoke-grey ceiling. Instead he merely hauled his big octagonal-barrelled Colt .45 and cocked the hammer.

The effect of this stunned the locals. For vicious Wheeler and knife-artist Creek both instantly fell back into their chairs just like men who genuinely feared they might be shot where they sat – a very distinct possibility when Holly was around. For what seemed an eternity nobody dared move or eat, until a yellow-eyed Holly at last eased the hammer down on the revolver he'd drawn and cocked, then shoved the piece back into its cutaway holster.

Moodily then, still without speaking, he began gnawing on his big shinbone again and it was a signal. One by one his henchman resumed the eating, griping and cussing that they had been enjoying before, and a tense calm seemed to settle.

Behind his counter, the greasy Mex proprietor wiped cold sweat off his shining face and prayed in

Spanish. He watched enviously when three local hardcases eased to their feet and slunk out, wishing he could do the same – which he would if he wasn't so afraid they might burn his place down. Where in the name of Saint Theresa was the law when an honest man really needed it? These wild-looking *hombres* looked as though they would steal the pennies from a blind man's eyes.

'So?' Holly Platte grunted upon finally finishing his frugal meal. The boss of the wildest bunch of thieves and killers ever to come out of the Burning Hills was a sparing man with the words. Then, 'So . . . what?' he barked when nobody responded.

Tom Morgan felt it might be up to him to oblige. Sawn-off, wild-eyed and ugly as sin, Morgan was the bunch's top trailsman and sign-reader. As he'd failed to come up with the scent of the man who'd gunned down Aaron Platte in Toryville, Morgan's standing with the gang boss had slumped dangerously with the gang boss recently.

'I figure that varmint must've took to the mountains and headed direct for Mexico right after shootin' good old Aaron down,' he opined in his whining nasal drone. 'If we really want to nail that butcher then I reckon we gotta be prepared to make for the border.'

'*If?*'

Again it was just a single word Holly dropped, but it packed weight. For Aaron had been his protégé, the only one of his three brothers who'd shown signs of developing into the kind of feared man killer which Holly Platte was proud to be.

'Yeah, Holly,' Morgan said, flushing a little. 'I say we oughta head for Mexico right away, man.'

'Shell?' Holly queried.

Cleat Shell, beetle-browed and with a strangler's hands, was smarter than he appeared. 'That there trail is cold as a week-dead cow, Holly,' he stated flatly. 'The only thing as I see it now is for us to fan out wide as we can spread and just keep crossin' and criss-crossin' until somebody cuts this geezer's sign.'

Bill Gannon made to speak but the leader silenced him with an upraised hand. For Shell's plan jelled with the leader's own thinking on what should be done, which was all he'd wanted to hear. Clearing the table with a sweep of the arm that set up a deafening clatter of smashing cutlery and crockery, the outlaw leader then tossed the contents of a full sugar bowl across the table and straightaway began sketching in it with his forefinger.

'This is us,' he grunted, gesturing. 'Heartbreak Valley to the west, the Breaks country east, badlands and the Snow Wolf Mountains south. Shell, you'll take your boys and go east, while Tom, Barney, Conway and Huck head south and the others take the west. If we don't cut sign then we'll meet back here in five days time. Anybody gets a whiff of this

68

butcher, wire through here to the post office. Any questions?'

Barney Platte had one. 'What if we flush him, Holly? What do we do?'

'What the hell do you think?' came the terse reply. 'We kill the murderin' son of a bitch, is what.'

'Like the kid tried to do?' Barney queried significantly.

Silence fell. For this was a telling point. The youthful Aaron Platte had been freely considered as fast as any man in the bunch. It was a combination of vanity and gunspeed that had prompted the man to challenge Clay Bodie at Toryville. Bodie had beat him to the draw and shot him stone dead, so Barney felt entitled now to ask that big question: 'What if we flush him?'

Holly Platte brooded over his maps for a spell. Until that moment the killer had refused to concede that the quarry they were hunting might be genuinely dangerous. But now with the gang about to split up in order to press on with the search, this was plainly a factor to consider. It galled Platte to concede that any man might be his better with the Colts, but this man Bodie had surely staked out some sort of a claim in that direction recently.

He rose and straightened.

'All right. Any man who flushes him will hot-foot it to the nearest telegraph station and wire the news back to this dump, then keep tabs on Bodie until all of us get back to the sightin' point. That way we'll all take him together.

Heads nodded soberly. But at least one hardcase had his fingers crossed. Only a year had separated Huck and Aaron Platte. They'd grown up like twins, had fought together, robbed stages side-by-side, shared dreams of outlaw glory. If there had been one area of conflict for the brothers it was the fact that Aaron had always been seen as the coming gun champion by big brother Holly, so Huck had to be content with third place in the pecking order.

This had never sat well with Huck Platte, and he admitted as much when he rode out with Morgan, Conway Burns and Barney some time later.

'Seems to me if any man gets to cut Bodie's trail, he should try to nail the varmint before he ups and mebbe disappears on 'em, Barney.'

'You heard what Holly said.' Barney's tone warned against further discussion.

One hour later the youngest surviving Platte was still sulking as they topped out a crest in the trail which afforded their final backwards glimpse of distant Yellow Gulch.

Well to the east now, Cleat Shell and his three riders were already fording Sundown River at the same hour Holly Platte and his gun crew were just clearing the town and heading west.

It was a time-honoured custom in the bunch never to pay for grub, and although he'd supplied a stack of meals and lost plenty crockery that day, the shaking Mexican cook was at that point in time pouring himself a triple rye whiskey and assuring himself he'd come out of the whole thing cheap – considering.

The visitors to Yellow Gulch had not identified themselves; there was no need. Holly Platte's gaunt likeness decorated the West from a thousand true-bills posted throughout Colorado, but no bounty man in his right mind would dare go hunting that one.

The lights of the town winked at them briefly then were cut off from sight as the party headed downs-lope from the high crest, riding Indian file now. Overhead, brilliant western stars blazed down, ahead lay wild and broken country stretching away into the hazy distances where gaunt hilltops fanged the horizon.

This was new country to all but Morgan the trails-man, and after they'd covered yet another rocky mile, big Barney griped, 'Pretty lousy country, Tom. Anythin' down below but more dust and heat?'

'Mighty little of anythin' for the next forty to fifty miles,' Morgan admitted. 'But once beyond Heart-break Hills we hit the fringe of the cattle range country. Reckon we'd better check out the spreads and the town out there before we push on to the Snow Wolfs.'

'They got telegraph at this here crummy town?' Huck Platte wanted to know.

'Sure thing,' said Morgan.

'So, what's this dump called,' asked Barney.

'Big Bend.'

Attorney Ingersole stood stiff and correct in a tight brown suit, his lawyer's pince-nez perched on a long nose catching the light as the general's coach and outriders swung into view from Lee Street.

The attorney checked himself out in a wall mirror to make certain he presented just the right mix of sober sympathy and business-like efficiency that he felt the occasion demanded. Satisfied with what he saw, he flicked a speck of dust from a lapel then turned to face the door.

A bunch of citizens was on hand to witness the arrival of Judah Richter's carriage that morning, for it was widely known in Big Bend that today was the day Blayney West's will was to be read.

The general opinion was that Blayney would not have left his good widow much of anything apart from a good stack of bills. Yet rumours of a gold strike and a 'secret map' were persisting, guaranteeing a good turnout.

Heads nodded in approval as the carriage halted and the general himself gallantly helped the widow down.

The general had been Carrie West's constant companion since her husband's death and it was suspected by some that his interest in the young widow might be more than that of a mere friend.

Around the long bars and cracker barrels of Big Bend they were already match-making busily, and the majority felt that should the general decide to marry, he couldn't do better than trade vows with Carrie West.

It seemed fitting to many that Big Bend's patron and leading citizen and the town's most eligible widow should marry – after a suitable and proper mourning period, of course.

Sheriff Sadler nodded to the general and Carrie fell in alongside Reb Quent as they descended the steps. Attorney Ingersole greeted them soberly, assured the widow it was a sad and solemn occasion, then conducted them into his large, gloomy office which smelt of dust and ancient law books.

When all were seated, Ingersole went behind his desk and picked up the document which was Barney West's last will and testament, cleared his throat importantly.

'Mrs West, General—'

That was as far as he got as the latecomer came through the doors. Everybody turned, and Richter muttered a soft curse when he realized who it was. He instantly caught Sadler's eye, for this was plainly a matter for the law to handle.

Sadler moved towards the dark-garbed figure with some hesitancy. Though the gunfighter had kept out of trouble here his ongoing presence ruffled nerves.

'What are you doin' here, mister?' he demanded quietly.

Bodie put a hard eye on Carrie West then fingered back his hat. 'What everyone else is doing . . . that's if it's all right by you.'

'Of course it isn't all right. These good folk are gathered here to hear the readin' of Blayney West's will, and your presence here is—'

He broke off. Bodie had made himself comfortable leaning back against the wall. The sheriff flushed hotly and swung to look at the general. Richter spoke to Quent who rose eagerly, but then halted when Ingersole found his voice again.

'For pity's sake,' he reproved, 'let us have no disturbances here. That would be almost blasphemous.'

'I've got an interest here,' Bodie stated calmly, his gaze flicking at the pale-faced girl. 'You see, I've found out that Blayney could have gone directly from your house to the saloon the day he came after me, General, and even a gunfighter likes to know why somebody wanted to murder him.'

The silence that ensued was thick and seemed to possess a weight of its own.

It was broken at last by the pale-faced widow. 'Oh, for heaven's sake, let him stay. Please continue, Mr Ingersole.'

As anticipated, Blayney West's worldly possessions proved to be meagre and of very limited interest – until the map surfaced.

Turned out the deceased had left this item in a long manilla envelope which Ingersole passed to the widow. The envelope contained a map drawn by her late husband detailing a section of mountain terrain not specifically identified by name.

By the time the buzz of curiosity had died down, the general had offered to take care of the map on the widow's behalf to save her having to worry about it. To the surprise of all, and particularly the general – or so it seemed to an attentive Bodie – the bereaved woman declined the offer, and secured the map in her pocketbook.

'I'll study it later,' she stated, with a grimace. 'Knowing Blayney's terrible luck with his work and such matters, I'm pretty certain this will prove worthless . . . like all the other maps at home, but then it can be kept safe in the bank.'

'Of course . . . as you wish, Carrie,' the general said stiffly, but said no more as Ingersole wound up the reading, then announced that all the legalities had been discharged. Meeting over.

They filed out. Bodie crossed to the hitch-rail and selected a cigar from his case. The others gathered in knots, stealing offended glances at him for his presence on such an occasion, though he sensed Carrie West's annoyance seemed tinged by something like curiosity, until Richter took her by the arm and escorted her to her covered carriage.

Attorney Ingersole emerged last of all, sniffing as he

passed the gunfighter and toting the will in his hand.

Bodie was considering all he'd seen and heard as he ground out his part-smoked stogie and swung into the saddle. It was only as he turned the sorrel towards the gates that he saw his way appeared blocked by a number of men as Richter spoke to his driver and rumbled away.

As Quent's men drifted away, the sheriff approached the gunfighter; his manner looked at the same time hesitant yet determined.

'Rather poor taste, Bodie.' The lawman's voice sounded dry.

'What?'

'Your showin' yourself at such a time. Don't you reckon you've raised enough dust here?'

Bodie drew good cigar smoke deep into his lungs. 'I guess you think high of Carrie West, Sheriff?'

'Of course I do.'

'And of the general, too?'

'The general is the very backbone of Big Bend.'

'But not a man without enemies, so I hear tell.'

'What's that meant to mean?'

Bodie considered the glowing tip of his cigar. 'Isn't it true that he and Blayney West didn't see eye to eye?'

'You can't expect any man to get along with everybody.'

'That doesn't answer my question.'

'Just what are you drivin' at, gunfighter?'

'Blayney West and Richter were at odds as I hear it, lawman. Yet I've reason to believe West was with Richter the day I shot him. Doesn't that strike you as curious?'

Sadler frowned. 'Maybe it would . . . if it was so.'

'Somebody gave Blayney West the idea that it was me who killed his sister. Nobody recollects West saying anything about me before I showed up here, so I calculate that he wasn't told I'd killed the woman until that morning. And that morning, *he* was up on Richter Hill!'

'Just what are you hintin' at, Bodie?'

'That Richter or somebody up there lied to him.'

'Why would they do that?'

'That's what I'm asking you. We know West thought the world of his sister, and he had a trigger temper. Whoever spun him that big lie would have been dead-set sure he'd come gunning for me – and most likely get himself killed. So, who would want Blayney West dead that bad?'

Sadler shook his head. 'Nobody that I know of.'

'Then we'll wait and see.'

'You mean to stay on?'

'Yeah.'

'Why? So you can cause more trouble?'

'I don't want trouble, Sheriff,' Bodie said quietly. 'Maybe if I can find out who sent West to go against me, and why, then folks might change their minds about me.'

Sadler exhaled a long breath. 'Why this town, Bodie? Why did you have to pick Big Bend, damn you?'

'Maybe I just took a shine to folks here,' Bodie smiled sardonically. Then seriously, 'They could just get to know me and even accept me, given half a chance.'

Sadler was sour as he watched the gunfighter walk away, then turned towards his office with a heavy tread.

Life had seemed uncomplicated before Bodie, he brooded. The general had bossed a model town, which was exactly what Big Bend had been before the gunfighter came. Everybody had been on edge ever since West was shot down, with the bookmaker now laying odds that Bodie would either quit town of his own accord, be run out by the mineral, or kill somebody else.

Perhaps the lawman could live with that. But what disturbed him deeply was the fact that Bodie had demanded to know if anybody would have cause to wish Blayney West dead. This had caused Sadler to recall immediately those rumours that Richter was in love with Carrie Bodie, and he muttered bitterly as he mounted the steps that took him inside where he tied into the deputy for failing to sweep out the office during his absence.

His attack made the deputy feel bad, yet the sheriff's mood began to improve a little. But even with time it would have no effect in dispersing that unwelcome seed of suspicion Clay Bodie had sown in his mind . . . a seed destined to bear bitter fruit.

CHAPTER 6

SWEET LUCY

The lamplighter was making his rounds that evening as the northbound stage rolled noisily in from Tolliver. The high-wheeled coach brought in a sack of mail, a satchel for the bank, Doc Monroe's fresh supplies of drugs – and just a single passenger who squinted from the coach window from puffy eyes.

'Big Bend!' bawled driver Henry Wintergreen, slamming on the brake as he swung the team into the depot landing. 'All out for Big Bend – ten minutes before we leave for the north!'

'He's been hollerin' thataway three times a week ever since the day I showed up here two years ago,' complained Manny Martin from his regular bench beneath the cottonwood tree close by. Manny had already been drunk twice that day but had kept swill-ing the suds manfully to drink himself relatively sober again. 'The loudest hog-caller and worst driver in Colorado Territory – that's our Henry.'

The drunk was a voluble character himself. His voice carried on this occasion and the driver swung angrily at the remark, but his annoyance vanished when he realized who it was seated at Martin's side in the tree shadows.

'Damned old lush!' Wintergreen muttered, then went to get the stage door and swung it open with a flourish. 'Down you get, Miss Lucy, ma'am. Hope the ride wasn't too rough on you?'

The woman who stepped down was around twenty but appeared much older. Her dress was too tight, her hemline too high, the bright paint she wore far too gaudy to be either youthful or ladylike. Yet the face underneath all the cosmetics was pretty enough and the blonde curls tended to offset the greedy hardness of her red-painted lips.

Lucy Doolin had never been to Big Bend before and was dabbing at her eyes while the driver lifted her valise down from the roof rack, before asking him where she might locate the West home.

Standing in the leafy shade of the cottonwood, Clay Bodie halted the cigar he was smoking before it reached his lips.

'First turn on your left, then the third house along, Miss Lucy,' the driver replied. 'Can't miss the widow's house on account it's the neatest on the street.'

She failed to thank the man; manners weren't Lucy's long suit. Sniffing and dabbing at her eyes she started off towards the Lee Street corner, but halted when a man rose from the bench to block her path.

'Tote your bag, miss?' Bodie offered.

The girl frowned at first, then paused to look him up and down. She smiled wanly. 'Why, yes, if you want to, handsome.'

'Clay Bodie's the name,' he said, taking the valise.

She flinched as though he'd struck her. 'You?' she gasped. 'You're the one who murdered him. You killed my Blayney!'

Bodie halted. He couldn't deny the charge. But he'd deliberately encountered the girl after being informed who she was. He was vitally interested in anyone who might have connections with Carrie West. '*Your* Blayney?' he queried.

The girl seemed genuinely distressed. Trembling hands raised to her face and real tears filled her eyes. But Bodie stared at her without sympathy. He had to be rock hard if he wanted to find answers to a lot of big questions in this town.

'What's your business with Carrie West?' he demanded. When this failed to draw a response he turned and imperiously beckoned the stage driver across. Wintergreen acted cautious as an old dog in long-grass snake country as he approached.

'Yeah, Mr Bodie, sir?'

'You know this woman?'

'Why, sure, she's Lucy Doolin from Tolliver.'

'Saloon girl?' Bodie guessed as Lucy blew her nose.

'Yeah, Mr Bodie. Used to work over at the Lucky Dollar.'

'So, what's she doing back here?'

Wintergreen looked uncomfortable. The scene was attracting bystanders who strained forward in the hope of overhearing what was going on.

'I don't rightly know as how I should say any more, Mr Bodie.'

'I asked a question and I want an answer,' came the sharp retort. Earlier, he'd overheard a couple of loafers speaking of the girl's expected arrival and hinting at her connection with the deputy, which had caused his ears to prick sharply.

The stagecoach man shrugged and leaned close to Bodie to whisper, 'She used to be West's gal, Mr Bodie. Seems to me she mighta shown up here in the hope he might've left her somethin' to remember him by, you know?'

'Is this so?' Bodie demanded, turning back to her.

Lucy dried the crocodile tears and talked straight. 'Of course it's true. And I ain't ashamed either. Blayney and I were always close even when he was chasing after her for money and—'

'Get about your business!' Bodie barked as he swung upon the curious bystanders. 'This has nothing to do with any of you.'

A brave citizen might have demanded to know what it had to do with him, but there were few heroes in this tough town.

They all drifted away until only Wintergreen and Manny Martin were left as Bodie returned his attention to the painted girl, tearless now and seemingly composed as she met his stare.

'Keep talking,' he ordered, knowing he was grasping at straws here, but straws were all he had.

'We were lovers,' she declared willingly, even proudly. 'He was fixin' to leave his wife and take me to Mexico after he finished with the mine—'

'What mine?'

Her look turned crafty. 'That's a secret.'

His eyes glittered as his hand rested on gunbutt. 'I said – what mine, Lucy?'

He'd succeeded in genuinely scaring her he realized when she shed some genuine tears at this point. She dabbed at her eyes and he almost felt sorry for her. Almost.

'Please,' she breathed, 'you wouldn't kill me *too*, would you?'

'Only if you make me,' he stated convincingly. 'I want to hear about this mine, Lucy,' he added, still grabbing at straws. 'So tell me quick before I do something we'll both be sorry for.'

He was proving too convincing an actor for this tough chippy. Before, she had been faking fear; now he really had her scared. 'The Lost German,' she breathed.

'That's just a myth!' he accused.

'No it isn't. Blayney stumbled on it months ago . . . there was a map. . . .'

His eyes widened. 'A map? So, that's what you're after here?'

'Yes!' she said defiantly. 'And I have a right to what Blayney found. He loved me and he didn't love that stuck-up tart. I've a right!'

'Women who steal other men's husbands don't have any rights in my book, lady.' He glanced at Wintergreen. 'How long before this stage leaves for the north, pilgrim?'

'Ten minutes' stop-over, Mr Bodie, about three minutes from now.'

'What's the fare to the next town?'

'Seven dollars even.'

'Here's ten,' he said, shoving a hand into his pants pocket as he turned to the puzzled girl. 'Your ticket's bought and paid for as of *now*, Lucy. That widow woman's got all she can carry right now without you fouling things up. Here's her freight, driver. See she stays on until Storyville or I'll come after you.'

'You know, if it comes right down to cases, I figure she can easy afford to pay her own freight, Bodie,' Wintergreen advised. 'On account she is really loaded.'

'You've got money?' Bodie demanded.

'That's my business,' Lucy retorted, regaining some of her fiery spirit now.

'How much?' Bodie insisted, hard and suspicious.

'A heap,' Wintergreen insisted.

'Show me that purse,' Bodie ordered, and when the girl hesitated, he plucked the purse from her arm and snapped open the catch.

The purse was packed solid with greenbacks.

He raised his gaze slowly to her face. 'Where did you get all this money, Lucy? You steal it?'

'I'm no thief!' she said defiantly. 'That money was given to me.'

'By who?' he demanded toughly. 'Blayney West, maybe?'

'What of it? He loved me and wanted me to have it—'

'Where did *he* get it?' Bodie demanded, but then had to drop a hand on to gunbutt to secure his answer.

'I told you he found the Lost German Mine,' Lucy declared. 'Blayney brought the first batch of gold down from the hills a month ago . . . three thousand dollars' worth.'

'You're saying West died rich?'

'He would have been rich if you hadn't killed him, you cold-blooded bastard!'

He'd been called worse things than that in his life. He passed the bag back to her, rested hands on hips.

'All right, girl, maybe I believe you, maybe not.

Just one more question before you leave.'

'Who says I'm leavin'?'

'We both know you've got to go. And you will stay gone and keep that pretty mouth shut tight – right?'

He radiated menace in that moment. She swallowed painfully, the last of her shallow courage deserting her entirely now.

'Yes,' she breathed unevenly. 'I-I don't want trouble with a killer.'

He flinched at that, but ground on regardless. 'The question, girl. Do you know who might have wanted Blayney dead?'

'No, I don't. But I know he was scared – really scared. He believed there was someone here who knew about the mine, even though he did everythin' he could to keep it secret.'

'But you don't know who this somebody was?'

'No, on account Blayney didn't know either. But there was somebody.'

Bodie nodded slowly. 'All right, that'll do it. So long, Lucy. Have a good trip.'

It was ten o'clock before Bodie completed his letter to Captain Frank Chase in Denver.

The communication was brief but to the point.

Bodie was seeking information on the wartime career and general background of General Judah Richter, formerly of Sherman's Army of the Union. As a career officer and War Office expert, he reckoned the captain would be certain to have records on such a distinguished soldier as Richter, and as a friend of Clay Bodie's of many years' standing, he would feel obligated to furnish such information promptly as requested.

Bodie hauled the postmaster out of bed to take his letter, then drifted off down Abraham Street until reaching the bottom of the trail leading up to Richter Hill.

It had been a long and testing day, he mused, but eventful and culminating in Miss Lucy Doolin's brief yet revealing visit.

He'd warned Wintergreen and Martin against revealing anything that may have transpired at the depot. He doubted if either man would find himself able to keep silent indefinitely, but was counting on Manny's chronic drunkenness and general befuddlement, and Wintergreen's reputation as a reckless gossip, to ensure that their strange story, should it leak out, would be treated with scepticism.

He felt it would be both easy and likely for Big Bend to discount any rumour relating to the fabled if probably mythical Lost German Mine. He would have found it hard to swallow this himself had he not glimpsed that fat wad of notes in Lucy Doolin's purse.

He still wasn't certain he believed the story completely himself.

The legend of the Lost German Mine dated back

many years ago long before the Civil War. The 'German' of the legend was some crazy old migrant who was rumoured to have struck it rich somewhere high in the Snow Wolf Mountains, where he'd been prospecting unsuccessfully for many years hitherto, before suffering a fatal heart attack on his last journey back to civilization for supplies.

The myth-makers had it that a poke containing a thousand dollars' worth of dust was found on the body, along with a map of the mine's location, which was subsequently lost.

For years afterwards, prospectors from all over the West had combed the Snow Wolf Mountains in a vain search for the mine, many perishing in the bitter cold or at the hands of hostile redskins.

Since those days, nothing appeared to have been added to the story – until the sundown stage from Tolliver had brought a red-lipped saloon girl with a purse filled with money and a tale about a map. . . .

The lights from Richter's Hill glowed brightly now against the purple background of the night sky as Bodie stood with arms folded and a frown cutting his dark brows.

He'd learned plenty about Richter since his arrival – a renowned soldier who'd made his reputation in battle, then earned himself a fortune in Mexico as a soldier of fortune before returning to settle down in Big Bend, Colorado, where he'd used his money to breathe new life into a hitherto dying community.

Although hard and uncompromising in his ways, Richter was plainly highly regarded with all but a few of the Manny Martin breed. Surely, it seemed fanciful to entertain the thought that a man such as Richter might be involved in anything underhand?

Yet stroking his neatly trimmed moustache, Bodie was conscious of doubts working the back of his mind.

The stones in Blayney West's horse's hoofs suggested that Blayney had been up on Richter Hill the day he died . . . there was Richter's obvious infatuation with Carrie West . . . the boss man's offer to hold on to the map left in Blayney West's will and his obvious anger when this offer was rejected. . . .

Could all these things suggest that the general knew about the Lost German Mine, that he may have plotted to get Blayney West out of the way, leaving himself free to lay claim to both West's widow and his goldmine?

He blinked at the enormity of this wild thought, then rejected it with an impatient grunt. A certain breed of operator might plot and act in such a way to gain his own ends, but not men like the general. There had to be another explanation.

His wandering steps led him to Lee Street. From the shadow of a big old elm he found himself gazing across at the white-painted cottage and felt some kind of tightness in his chest.

He smiled a bitter smile of self-knowledge. Here,

alone, he didn't have to pretend he was staying on at this place for any reason other than the real one. Not that he was simply weary of running, or because he needed to find out why Blayney West had braced him that day.

Here, in the velvet softness of the Colorado night, Clay Bodie, the gunfighter with the quiet conscience, could admit he'd fallen in love for the first time in his life and could further acknowledge that in doing so, he must be the greatest fool unhung. . . .

He suddenly felt better, realizing he was being honest with himself for the first time since riding into this town. And having done this now, he was able to look at the situation calmly and honestly and reach a decision.

He would wait until he received his reply from Frank Chase, he decided, and if the report on the general was clear and straightforward, then he would quietly saddle up and quit, knowing he had done all he could and should for the woman he'd fallen in love with.

He felt saddened yet secure in his decision as he walked on. But for Carrie West, he knew he would have made a greater effort to stay on here, for he knew he was weary to death of the endless running, and there was something about Big Bend and its people that had captured his fancy, despite the antagonism towards him.

But it would be impossible to stay on now, seeing

her, wanting her, having her as a constant reminder of a quiet and regular world such as could never be his.

He expected his reply from the north within the week. He could endure Big Bend for that time he assured himself, unaware that even as he reached this decision Destiny was formulating its own plans for Clay Bodie in the shape of a wild boy with a gun, every moment even now drawing swiftly closer and closer to Big Bend on flying pony hoofs.

CHAPTER 7

NONE SO VAIN

A tarnished yellow sun was blazing down on Big Bend as Clay Bodie sat in the Tambourine Saloon sipping Old Atlanta whiskey and listening to the shouting from the street of the man out there who wanted to kill him.

It was cool in the Tambourine with the shutters closed tight against the summer glare. Upon the long shelves of the bar, bottles of amber and gold gleamed cool and inviting.

Off to one side, a bunch of five men sat about the faro layout, their hands still now with cards and chips lying idle as the players also listened to that strident voice from Abraham Street . . . and wondered what the dark-eyed man in the black leather vest might do.

Over at the piano Professor Gus Erwin played a

little louder in an unsuccessful attempt to drown out the insults which came floating in over the batwings. Behind his bar, and sweating far more than the day's heat warranted, saloon-keeper Clint Weller debated whether simply to close up shop, attempt to persuade Bodie to leave by the rear – or maybe go take a switch out to young Rooney Van and apply it to where it would do the most good.

'So . . . where is that wild and woolly gunfighter? Hey, Bodie! What are you doin'? Searchin' for your guns in a whiskey glass, maybe?'

The taunts grew stronger as Rooney Van gained confidence. It was blistering hot out on Abraham Street, where for several tense minutes now the would-be gunslinger had had its broad and dusty length all to himself.

Following each new challenge hurled through the open windows of the Tambourine, the young gunslinger would look up and down Abraham to see pale faces staring from windows and doorways, some admiring, some fearful, yet all transfixed by the drama being played out before their eyes.

The kid was proud of the way he was performing, yet also a little puzzled. Where was the general and his men? The last time when Rooney had sought to add another scalp to his trophy belt, the general had dispatched four of his men to bundle the county's youngest gunslinger out of town.

Van had expected Richter to intervene today, but

so far nothing had happened.

There was only one way to interpret this, and that was that Richter had finally realized that Van was far too dangerous to tangle with. Rooney could only hope the famous gunfighter didn't share the general's fear of him. The fast gun felt ten feet tall today and believed nothing short of an avalanche could bring him down.

He struck a pose by the water trough and hollered at the top of his lungs, 'Come on out, Grandpa, or do you want me to send a wheelchair in to carry you out?'

His grin became a chuckle. That was pretty good. He was having a high old time.

Bodie had not moved since the first shout reached him. He was willing both the voice and its owner to vanish, but wasn't holding out any real hope. This breed had never acted sensibly in his experience at other places. Why should things be any different here in this strange Colorado town? Gun punks were gun punks every place you went.

He stared at the wall before him and the remoteness that was part of him seemed all the more evident now.

Eventually, slowly now, as if the simple act of moving demanded considerable effort, he turned to face that rear doorway. The green painted door stood partly opened to the galley passageway. There was nothing to prevent him simply walking out. But he knew that the big-mouthed kid in the street would settle for nothing less than a showdown, if not here, then wherever he might choose to run.

So then – it might as well be here.

The gunfighter's dark eyes returned to the saloon-keeper. 'Who is it, Weller?' He spoke without emotion.

'Rooney Van. They call him Wild Rooney.'

'He sounds like a kid.'

'He is. But one mighty mean kid, Mr Bodie. He's killed two men here that I know of.'

'So, a punk kid hunting gun notches?'

'I reckon that fits him right enough.'

'Where's that big man who's supposed to lord it over all this?'

The barkeep affected not to hear. 'Rooney shot a drunk in a brawl about six weeks back, then killed some drifter a short time later. He's been drivin' folks loco with his braggin' and carryin' on ever since. But I guess you'd know that kind?'

Bodie nodded grimly, while from the street came another strident yell.

'Bodie! Do you want for me to come in there and drag you out by that famous long hair of yours?'

'I don't reckon he'll go away, Mr Bodie,' said Weller.

No response.

'There's a couple of good mounts in the stables in back, Mr Bodie. You could just saddle up and ride out.'

It was at this point that a faint suspicion entered Bodie's mind. Might not this whole thing have been staged simply to get rid of him? He shook his head after a moment. Surely not. That kid out there sounded genuine, not somebody merely playing some dumb game.

The rear door swung open.

The barman gasped at the speed with which Bodie whipped out his Colt and whirled to face the rear. Slowly Bodie straightened when he recognized the red-faced Deputy Rube Tancred.

Contempt curled Bodie's top lip as he spun the Peacemaker on his finger and dropped it back into the stiff leather holster. Tancred was scared. Bodie could smell his fear at thirty feet.

'What the hell are you doing here, Deputy?'

Tancred approached as though his knees weren't working right.

'I don't want another killin' in this town, Bodie.'

'That's *Mister* Bodie. So, you can avoid a shoot-up by moving that punk off the street, Badgeman.'

'Me tangle with Wild Rooney the mood he's in? That'd be plain loco, Mr Bodie. I stopped by to kind of suggest you might like to maybe cut and drift before things come to gunsmoke.'

'Where in hell is the sheriff?'

'Don't know.'

'That figures.'

'What do you mean?'

'Never mind. Are you going to handle this matter or not?'

'I can't. He'd likely kill me.'

'Then get to hell and gone out of my sight!'

The deputy paled with twin spots of crimson burning sallow cheeks. He appeared scared, angry and offended all at once.

'Now see here, gunfighter—'

He broke off as Bodie's right hand seized a fistful of his shirt and twisted it chokingly tight.

'You likely just signed that kid's death warrant, Deputy!' he accused through locked teeth. 'Live with that!' He flung the man violently from him then swung about and strode for the batwings.

Van was strutting up and down across the main stem with little puffs of dust rising at his every step. He was a slimly built *hombre*, wore a broad-brimmed black hat and sported twin six-shooters thonged to his thighs.

Sensing the movement from the saloon he halted to face the batwings, his narrow, pinched faced flushed with liquor and venom.

'Bodie, is that you? Sure it is. So, come on out, old man and let's get this over with – neat, fast and permanent.'

For a dragging moment, Bodie stood motionless with his hands on the half-opened bat wings. It was as though there were no tense citizens in back of him, no fearful faces watching from all along the street.

Nothing but Clay Bodie and this sharp-faced kid.

His brain seemed to be working sluggishly. How many Rooney Vans would this make? How often had he played his part in dramas exactly like this? He'd always fought against keeping count, and had partly succeeded. But though the precise number might be dim, faces and names were branded in his memory just the same.

Was there now to be a new addition . . . the unremarkable name of Rooney Van?

He threw the batwings wide and stepped out into the sun.

Across the street, his sudden appearance caused Rooney Van a fierce jolt of misgiving when he realized that Bodie seemed to fit his reputation so impressively.

The supple slope of the shoulders, the smooth implacability of the expressionless features above that neatly trimmed moustache and the sheer impression of latent power of the man. Van saw it all, was impressed far more than he wanted to be, yet hid his feelings behind a convincing snarl.

'You the geezer what's got 'em all walkin' on egg shells hereabouts, old man? Holy Judas, but you sure don't look nothin' special to me!'

'I'm your worst nightmare, kid!' declared the gunfighter, wanting to bluff him in order not to be forced to gun him down. He came down the steps with a hot breeze tugging at his shoulder-length hair and stirring the silken moustache. 'I'm just too ornery and just too blamed fast for boys like you to have anything to do with, son. Can't you see that?'

A flicker of uncertainy crossed the gun-kid's big-nosed face at that, then was gone. 'Well, you're sure some talker, Bodie, I'll give you that,' he sneered. 'Well, guess old folks tend to get gabby, don't they?'

'I'd like to see you get to grow old,' Bodie responded, still coming on. 'Just hate to see you dig your own grave with your flapping mouth before you got to twenty-one.'

'That's close enough, Bodie!'

'You sound scared, kid. You've got good reason.'

'Don't come no closer!'

Bodie's step did not falter. The sunlight striking fire from his cartridge belt, boot-heels sinking in the powdery dust of Abraham Street, he kept walking deliberately towards the man he didn't want to kill.

'Stop, or I'll kill you, Bodie!'

'I was faster at your age than you'll ever be even if you reach a hundred, kid . . . *no!*'

His warning came too late.

Already the gun-boy was slashing at his hip, his whole body lithely involved in that killer-draw of his, and the Abraham Street onlookers reckoned that Rooney's draw was surely the fastest thing they'd ever seen.

Yet to the eagle eye of Clay Bodie, a man who knew the gun trade so well, it was a suicide draw, so fast

100

there was no hope of real accuracy. By contrast, Bodie's own draw and clear were faultless – a dip of the right shoulder, the reflexive whip of his hand and in that breathtaking instant the weapon reached level and the Colt muzzle was staring at Van while his gun was yet to reach firing level.

Bodie only had to squeeze trigger to blast the other into eternity.

But he didn't.

Unbelievably, he felt himself frozen by a sense of revulsion for what life was demanding he do yet again. He saw, not Rooney Van, but the faces of dead men he had slain, ghostly images, grey, ghastly and decomposed by the grave.

Van's gun exploded like a cannon.

The kid fired too fast. The slug missed Bodie by inches. He twitched violently, but even then did not fire. He was like two people, one standing here in this sunblasted streeet, the second Bodie standing off to one side watching it all with an air of detachment as though none of this had anything to do with himself.

Then Rooney Van steadied his smoking Colt with both hands and hot lead kissed the side of Bodie's skull.

He was stunned by the bullet graze and reeled backwards. Van triggered yet again, but once more his aim was wild with the slug snoring high over Bodie's head and whining harmlessly away.

Bodie triggered just the once. Rooney Van spun in a slow circle, his smoking revolver dropping from his grasp as he took a half-dozen jerky little steps before he fell on his back in the dust.

The gunfighter got up and moved slowly to reach the side of the boy who might have killed him. In death, Rooney Van no longer appeared fierce, menacing or contemptuous of old men of thirty. He looked like a kid who shaved but once a week, who should have been at home doing some simple household chores for his ma instead of lying stiff and stark in a dusty street.

Bodie moved off slowly, his motions deliberate and heavy. He touched his forehead and his fingers came away bloody. He doubted the crease was serious, yet the bullet's impact had stunned him with the result he had to concentrate on placing one foot ahead of the other as he walked.

Somehow he made his way to the alley between hotel and saloon before the sun suddenly pitched crazily in his sight. Wildly he clutched at a fence slat, but his hand found nothing but empty air.

He was stretched out motionless with blood soaking his hair when the first shocked towners reached his side.

Bodie came out of it slowly.

There were times when he was aware of movement and action around him in the fog, the murmur of voices seemingly coming from a vast distance. Then he would drift off again into a haze where nothing was clear, where he seemed suspended as in a dream.

But eventually he recovered sufficiently to be aware of gentle hands, sharp smells, and once, the clear clatter of foosteps.

He frowned in his semi-consciousness, trying hard to remember. Then he was recalling the crazy gunslinger, the fire lancing at him from the barrel, felt again the sharp jolt of pain in his head.

He sighed, relaxed, and drifted off into sleep again.

When he awoke next his head was crystal clear. He became aware he was lying in a small, neat room filled with delicate scents. Birds twittered beyond the windows. He heard the clip-clop sounds of a passing dray horse. The wind shifted and somewhere a windmill began to hum.

The pain hit then.

Pain was an old acquaintance and his body carried the scars as testimony. The ache in his skull was mild compared with some he'd endured. He realized his head was shrouded in tight strapping and his exploring fingers traced the bullet furrow above his left ear. Close . . . damned close. Had he stood against a genuine gunman he knew he would now be dead.

He shut his eyes.

Twice in the one week, he brooded. First Blayney West, then Rooney Van. He'd faced both as though

103

inviting the fatal bullets.

Had he grown so weary of killing that he secretly wanted to die?

He shook his head. No. It was not that he wished to die, just that he'd been loath to kill that boy. . . .

He seemed to doze until some small sound stirred him and his eyes snapped wide. Carrie West stood there reaching out and placing a cool hand on his forehead. She nodded approvingly as though unaware of his surprise.

'Much cooler than before,' she summarized. 'How do you feel?'

'How did I get here?' he countered.

'I had them bring you here,' she said crisply, impersonally.

He sat up sharply, then clenched both eyes shut as vivid lances of fire shot through his skull. 'You had them . . . bring me here?' he got out. 'You, of all people?'

'You had to be taken some place,' she replied. 'People weren't exactly fighting to take you in.'

'Reckon I can see why. But more than anybody else, you'd have had the best reasons to let me lie there.'

'I doubt I hate anybody that much.' Then she half-smiled. 'I find hate a difficult thing to sustain, Mr Bodie. Something I discovered for myself, is that it nurtures itself, say, like the way love does.'

'I wouldn't know about that,' he replied tersely.

He was staring out the window. 'I killed that kid.'

'Yes, you did. I happened to see what happened from the corner. I saw it all, as a matter of fact, certainly enough to realize you had no choice.'

'He's dead, just the same.'

'Rooney Van was doomed to a short life. Everybody said so. That boy was involved in violent scrapes almost since childhood. He certainly must have wished to die to go up against someone like you.'

'Sure . . . bracing me is like catching smallpox. You're sure gonna die . . . and it's one hell of a lot quicker.'

'You're a strange man. Outwardly you're arrogant and cold, but underneath you are a different man. I suspect I sensed that even the first day.'

'Is that why you had them bring me here to your house? Because you sensed my better nature and reckoned it might be worth encouraging?'

He couldn't keep the bitterness out of his voice. Sometimes gunplay left him untouched. Other times? Well, other times he might feel badly for weeks afterwards, months even.

'Why are you angry with me?' she asked after a short silence.

That took him off-guard and turned his emotions inward. Why indeed? But he knew the answer. He was angry with her simply because her strength and kindness made him acutely aware of just how wide was the chasm that separated them. The gunfighter and the lady. Chalk and cheese. He tried to muster anger against her but couldn't invoke it. She had extended a Samaritan hand to lonesome Clay Bodie, and he was in her debt. It was as simple or as complicated as that, and he must accept it.

'Sorry,' he said at last, and it was a hard thing to say. He glanced around the room. 'Better fetch my clothes so I can check out of here.'

'You're not moving until Doc Monroe says so, and he won't be back until this afternoon. You'll rest now and I'll have a meal ready for you when you wake up.'

'You're awful damn bossy, lady.'

'Yes,' she replied softly. 'Blayney used to say that also.'

'I-I didn't mean it serious.'

'Of course you didn't. Now get to sleep. If you don't rest I might have you on my hands indefinitely.'

He lay back and drew the crisp sheet up around his neck. He studied her with brooding dark eyes as she fussed about until the oval of her face began to blur in his vision. He muttered something she didn't catch and then the darkness engulfed him.

He slept.

He recognized the general's voice moments after the sounds of conversation awakened him. He was fuzzy for a time as he sat up in the cot to see a chink of light beneath the door. Straining his ears, he finally identified the other voice. It was Carrie, and the pair seemed to be arguing.

Swinging bare feet to the boards he rose, then waited for his head to stop spinning. Then he padded across to the window. Three horses stood tied to the fence and two men stood nearby in the half-darkness, smoking. One was Reb Quent.

He crossed to the door and paused to listen. After some moments he realized General Richter was objecting to Carrie opening her doors to 'that damned gunslinger with his squaw man's hair'. Further dialogue revealed the big man wanted Clay Bodie tipped out pronto – 'Before folks start to gossip' as he phrased it.

But Carrie West countered the general calmly and firmly, then went on to apprise her visitor that even should his presence here raise a scandal in town, she simply didn't much care.

He returned to his bed and was building a smoke when she opened the door a chink and peered in. 'Oh,' she said, coming in. 'I hope we didn't wake you.'

He shook his head then cocked his head at the sound of receding hoofbeats. 'The general didn't sound too pleased just now,' he remarked casually.

She stood by the bedside. 'Did you overhear what was being said?'

'Some of it. Sounds like you're not doing yourself any favours by having me here.'

'I can deal with Judah Richter.'

'He's a friend?'

'Yes.'

'But he wasn't a friend of your husband.'

'Who told you that?'

'Does it matter?'

'I suppose not.' She shrugged as she crossed to the side table to make a light. 'Blayney and Judah didn't get along. They were very different personalities.'

'Was that the only reason?'

Lamplight flooded her face as she turned to him. 'What other reason could there be?'

'You. Richter's in love with you.'

She stiffened. 'That's foolish talk, Mr Bodie.'

'It's true though, isn't it?'

'I loved my husband,' she stated firmly. 'And he loved me. That's all I have left, but it's enough. I shall always love him.'

Bodie glanced away, thinking of Lucy Doolin in her thirty-dollar shoes.

'I don't want to sound impolite, Mrs West, but you did mention something about supper. . . .'

She smiled, happy to be back on safer ground. 'I'll go heat up something. Doc Monroe looked in on you during the afternoon and said you need nourishment now.'

'You're real anxious to get me back on my feet. Right?'

'Why, naturally.'

'Well, if that's the case, I know I'd likely heal lots faster if you were to drop that "Mr Bodie" stuff. Try Clay.'

She flushed prettily and in that moment it seemed that for the first time the tensions of recent days were finally beginning to leave her.

'Very well – Clay. And you may call me Carrie.'

He watched her leave the room with her dark hair shining. And in bed, alone with his thoughts, Clay Bodie had that rare feeling, for him, of not being completely alone. In these last hot days of a Colorado summer. . . .

CHAPTER 8

KANGAROO COURT

There came a break in the conversation when Carrie West rose to clear away the supper things. Through the smoke haze of the fine cigar he'd just lighted, Judah Richter studied the young woman, struck as always by the grace and dignity of the most attractive female he'd ever known.

With dark hair piled high and the light from the softly shaded lamp enhancing her creamy complexion, the widow appeared even more desirable than usual tonight and he felt piqued that she seemed unaware of the significance of the occasion.

Richter had taken special pains in preparing for the evening. The rich man had shaved and dressed with meticulous care and, studying his erect, polished reflection in the mirror before he'd left home, was more than satisfied with what he saw.

He had driven down in his best surrey and, aware that Carrie despised Reb Quent, had taken the unprecedented step of leaving his burly bodyguard back at the mansion.

Yet it seemed that all his careful preparations, so far as he could assess up until now – all this had been for nought.

She had welcomed him in her customary formal fashion, promptly poured him a drink before supper then served a meal just as though this night wasn't intended to be anything special.

But of course it was, and he decided it was high time she was made aware of it.

'Carrie,' he said soberly, leaning across the table, 'there's something important I must discuss with you.'

'Yes, Judah?'

He glanced at the partially opened doorway. 'Are you certain that damned gunslinger can't overhear us?'

'Clay is out on the back porch. And I do wish you wouldn't refer to him that way.'

Richter's lips pursed but he refused to become annoyed. Instead he tugged down his lapels and launched into a carefully prepared speech. He realized her husband, Blayney, was only recently deceased, but circumstances were forcing him to bring forward something that had been long on his mind, much earlier than he might otherwise have wished.

He began by revealing his sensitivity to what a testing life it must be on the frontier for any woman suddenly bereft of husband and provider, as Carrie most tragically had been. . . .

It took him some time to get to the point, but then he did so bluntly. Might she consent to become his wife?

Carrie was flattered, a little confused, yet quite firm. She deeply appreciated all the general had done for her, valued his friendship highly, yet the answer was, most emphatically, no.

Richter was stunned. He considered himself the most eligible man in the entire county. He was wealthy and cultivated and might very well become a United States senator. He was offering an impoverished widow a life that most women in her current position would gladly give their eye teeth to have.

And yet she was rejecting him.

'Why, woman?' he demanded. 'Is it because it's too soon after losing your husband? If so, I can be patient.'

'That is certainly part of the reason, Judah—' She broke off to glance towards the next room, then added, 'But there are also other reasons. I'm sorry, I really am.'

All colour had slowly drained from Judah Richter's patrician features. He pricked his ears as he heard the creaking of the rocking chair coming from the back porch. The sound filled him with a sudden unreasoning anger as he sent his chair back with a crash and got to his feet.

'By God, I wouldn't have believed it!' he breathed. 'But now that I think about it, I realize I should have suspected there was something between you and that damned gunfighter right from the start, otherwise you would never have taken him in the way you did.'

He paused to jab an accusing finger across the table.

'I've noticed the way other women look at that man, Carrie – but *you*!'

'Stop it, Judah!' she said sharply, also rising now. 'What you're implying is absolutely ridiculous. I took Clay Bodie in because he was hurt and in need, not for any other reason. I loved my husband and still do. There's no room in my life for any other man yet.'

'Prove it, Carrie.'

'What?'

Riding a lightning bolt of anger and emotion, Richter strode to the hat stand and snatched down his fine beaver. 'Get rid of him!' he almost shouted. 'Send him packing! If he's well enough to sit out on a porch he's well enough to move into a hotel. I want him gone by tomorrow!'

'I've never responded to ultimatums, Judah.'

'And I don't care for low gunfighters besmirching a fine lady's reputation and interfering with my personal plans. I'll be back here in the morning, Carrie. Make sure Bodie is no longer here, then we'll talk again.'

Her spirit showed as she said, 'I'm not sure there will be anything to discuss, Judah.'

'My dear,' he hissed, going out. 'You've never been more wrong!'

Doc Monroe said, 'You're healing mighty fast, young feller. . . .'

The medico paused as his knee made contact with the Colt jutting from his patient's holster.

'Will you get rid of that cussed contraption while I'm examinin' you? Damned if I'm anxious to get my toes blown off.'

'I never keep a bullet in the chamber, Doc.'

When Monroe stepped back from the chair with an expression of impatience, Bodie quickly smiled.

'All right, don't bust a blood vessel.' He hauled the .45 from its holster and placed it upon the low table by his chair. 'Happy now?'

'Guns!' the medico snorted. 'This world would be a far better place if they'd never been invented. All right, come over here and let me look at that there wound in the sunlight, damnit.'

Rising easily, Bodie did as instructed. It was the following day and he'd awakened feeling almost as strong as ever. He realized that from today he could no longer use his state of health as an excuse to

114

remain in the West home.

The medico turned his back to the window to check him out and so Bodie didn't sight the sheriff mounting the steps until it was too late.

Bodie stiffened at the sound of a gun hammer clicking and whirled to see Milt Sadler standing before him with a Colt .45 trained on his chest.

'What the hell—?' Bodie began, then twisted in the opposite direction at the sound of a startled cry. Recognizing Carrie West's voice he took one lunging step towards the door but froze as Reb Quent appeared in the doorway with a Colt in each fist.

Bodie's eyes went to his gun upon the table, then cut back to Monroe accusingly as the man backed up from him.

'Sorry, son,' the medico sighed, 'but I had to go along with the sheriff and get you separated from that hogleg of yours so there wouldn't be any gunplay.'

'Clay!' Carrie called from behind Quent. 'What's happening?'

'Bodie's under arrest, Mrs West,' Sadler informed her as Deputy Rube Tancred appeared around the corner of the house with a Winchester in his hands. The lawman was sombre as he jerked his chin towards the front. 'Let's go, gunfighter!'

'What's the charge, Sadler?'

'The murder of Rooney Van.'

'That was a fair fight.'

'You'll get your chance to prove that in court. Let's go.'

Bodie turned a blank look at Carrie as he went down the steps. This had to be some kind of macabre joke, he tried to tell himself as they walked towards the gate. Then he sighted the fine carriage drawn up across the street with General Richter's expressionless face staring out, and understanding struck like a body blow. The rich man had warned Carrie he wanted him gone from the house today – one way or the other. This was the pay-off. Bodie realized he was in deep trouble.

The trial in Big Bend of the People versus Clay Bodie got under way just an hour after word of the gunfighter's arrest swept through town with the speed of a brush fire. Big Bend was stunned and citizens flocked to the rickety courthouse to watch Judge Rushton preside over the presentation of evidence against the accused.

Rushton had retired years earlier but still travelled the circuit on occasion. He was a small, shrivelled individual with a great crown of silver-grey hair. He looked very dignified – and vaguely uncomfortable – as the witnesses paraded before him to present a damning picture of Clay Bodie gunning down Rooney Van 'like a dog in the street', as one anything but impartial witness phrased it for the benefit of the mob.

It was almost as if the judge realized that virtually

every word he heard was a lie, yet felt powerless to do anything about it. 'The People' were speaking.

Bodie made no attempt to defend himself.

From the moment he'd sighted the general's carriage outside Carrie West's house he'd known this would be a kangaroo court, with the general pulling the strings and his puppets dancing to his tune.

He was quickly proved right when Rushton and Sadler, along with the witnesses and the jury, all perjured themselves, with the inevitable result.

The verdict was a foregone conclusion.

The jurymen retired for less than ten minutes and the accused prisoner wondered bleakly why they had even bothered to leave the chamber at all before returning with a verdict of guilty. Not to murder, as charged, but to the lesser crime of manslaughter.

The courthouse was uncommonly quiet as they waited for the judge to hand down sentence, and to Clay Bodie it seemed that if anybody looked genuinely guilty here today it had to be those twelve good men and true, each one of whom now refused to meet his eyes.

His bleak gaze went to the rear of the court where the king of Big Bend sat with his retainers. Judah Richter had no hesitation in meeting Bodie's stare. The general's face, plain for all to see, wore an undisguised expression of triumph.

And Clay Bodie nodded understandingly to himself.

He'd fallen foul of the general and the power broker had brought him down. Simple as a fixed jury!

Yet gazing out over the sea of faces he sensed that the cost of this victory to the big man in town might prove higher than he'd planned.

Until today, Judah Richter appeared to have stood for peace, justice and liberty in this place. To the town he was the strong father-figure to whom lesser folk came with their problems and difficulties, and were sent away reassured and strengthened. Yet today, Bodie felt the general might well have slipped from his high perch, though judging by Richter's expression in that moment, he counted that cost as cheap.

The judge finally cleared his throat.

'Clay Bodie, you have been tried and found guilty of the heinous crime of manslaughter. Have you anything to say before I pronounce sentence?'

'Just one thing, old man. How will you sleep tonight?'

Rushton flushed deeply. 'On the charge of manslaughter I sentence you to five years' hard labour in the State penitentiary. Clear the court!'

Manny Martin gazed sympathetically at Clay through the bars. 'Want a slug, Bodie boy?' he invited, offering the brown bottle.

'Jumped up Judas, just what do you think this

118

place is, Manny?' protested Deputy Rube Tancred who'd just permitted the drunk to visit with his fellow inmate. 'Put that damned pint away right now!'

The drunk didn't respond swiftly enough and the deputy came forward and gave him a sharp clip with his night stick, just to remind him who was running this jailhouse.

Bodie growled, 'Leave the man be, Tancred.'

Tancred swung on the prisoner, unshaven jaw jutting aggressively. 'What did you say, Bodie?'

'You heard. Now get the hell back to your desk.'

Rube Tancred made a muttering sound in his throat and grabbed at his gun butt, yet there was confusion and uncertainty in his eyes. Bodie was unarmed and secure behind bars, which should mean Deputy Tancred had nothing to fear. But the longer he traded stares with the prisoner the less confidence he drew from either the touch of walnut under his fingers or those sturdy iron bars separating them.

'You won't walk so tall when you land in State Prison, gunslinger,' he warned feebly, turning away. 'They know just how to take care of your breed up there.'

'Go polish your badge, Rube,' snorted Manny, taking full advantage of the situation. He promptly proffered the bottle to Bodie again. 'Here you go, son. It'll help take away the taste of what they done to you today.'

'It'd take more than liquor to do that. Keep it for yourself, Manny.'

Swallowing a slug powerful enough to stiffen a Missouri mule, Manny Martin coughed, thumped his chest with his fist then reluctantly set the bottle aside.

'Like my old mammy used say, Bodie boy, drink don't solve your problems, just teaches 'em how to swim.' He hiccupped, then added in a stage whisper; 'You wanna bust outta here?'

'What?'

Manny winked broadly. Then reaching into the dank folds of his Confederate greatcoat, he calmly produced a fat little two-shot derringer. He shoved it through the bars at Bodie, who brushed the weapon aside.

'Where in hell did you get that thing, Manny?'

'Stole it from behind the bar at the Tambourine Saloon. Go on, take it, son.'

'No. Shove it away before Sadler sees it and jugs you, too.'

'You don't want to escape, boy?'

'Not that way.'

'How many ways are there? You've just been rail-roaded, Bodie boy, and if you don't do somethin' about it right quick they're gonna land you in State Prison. And there won't be anythin' even old Manny will be able to do for you once you wind up in that hell-hole.'

'Thanks – but no thanks, old-timer.'

The drunk he'd befriended before running foul of the law slipped his derringer away and took out his bottle again. 'You ain't throwin' in your hand, are you, son?' he asked anxiously.

The reason Bodie didn't reply was that he wasn't sure what his answer might be. He was a fighter by nature, but so many things had changed since that back trail had taken him to Big Bend. His refusal to accept that deadly little weapon and maybe get to blast his way out of this jailhouse, where he had no right to be, was a manifestation of just how much he'd changed over a short period of time.

Sure, he was embittered at the treatment he'd received. Yet oddly his resentment was directed at Richter alone, not at the lawmen or the citizens who'd helped put him here.

He still liked Big Bend and its people, still had that strong feeling it was a place where a man might set down his roots. But he couldn't take a gun to his jailers. They were simply the pawns of someone much stronger in Richter, and wouldn't stand a chance against him with a gun in his hand. He would sooner risk going to the Big House than shoot harmless citizens even if he bitterly loathed being caged.

The sheriff came in and ushered Martin out shortly afterwards, and some time later Tancred brought him in a pie that Carrie had baked.

He learned the girl had attempted to visit him here but Tancred had turned her away on the

121

grounds that it was against orders.

The implication had been that it was the sheriff's orders, but Bodie knew better. Judah Richter bossed the jailhouse like he did everything else. Which was why Bodie was under no misconceptions regarding the punishment he would receive. He'd intruded on what Richter regarded as his territory with the girl, and he must pay for that.

He fingered the calico strapping around his head and reflected on Carrie West's strength and tenderness. Lost in his reverie he was only vaguely aware at first of the rising sounds of confusion drifting in from the street. He came back to reality some time later when Sheriff Sadler and gambler Niles Strong came hurrying down the jailhouse corridor, both looking plenty worried.

'Bodie!' the sheriff barked without preamble. 'Just who in hell is after you?'

The prisoner blinked uncomprehendingly.

'Huh?'

'Who's doggin' you, dad-blame it, man? Niles here just come down from the north where he ran into these pilgrims who got to askin' questions about someone named Clay Bodie. They were as scary a bunch of hardcases Niles ever set eyes on, so naturally he blurted out where you was and—'

'What did they look like, Strong?' Bodie cut in sharply.

Strong supplied a description of the four

strangers, and it was Clay Bodie's turn to look grim. 'Huck and Barney Platte – and company!' he said bitterly.

'Platte?' The lawman's eyes opened wide. 'They any kin to Holly Platte?'

'His brothers,' Bodie confirmed. Then he added reluctantly, 'There was another brother, Aaron Platte. I killed him in a shoot-out in Toryville a month ago. I figured I'd shaken this pair off.'

Both men stared at him speechlessly. There was a wanted dodger out in the front office on Holly Platte, and Milt Sadler knew the charges against him off by heart: murder, kidnapping, cattle rustling, grand larceny, escaping lawful custody. If a crime could be committed, Holly Platte had seemingly done it. And Bodie had slain his brother.

The sheriff finally got his voice working again. 'They're heading this way?'

Bodie glanced across at the gambler. 'Thanks to your friend . . . nothing will stop them.' he paused, then added, 'You say there are only four, Strong?'

'I only seen four, Bodie. Could have been more, I guess.'

'How big is their bunch?' the sheriff wanted to know.

'Six, maybe seven men, at top strength.'

Bodie's words sounded like nails being hammered into the sheriff's coffin. He was holding prisoner a man being hunted by Holly Platte and his killer pack.

123

Milt Sadler simply wasn't equipped to handle a threat of that dimension. So, glassy-eyed and groggy, he went out, mounted up and rode up Richter Hill to confer with somebody who would tell him what he should do.

Bodie wasn't surprised when the sheriff returned an hour later with a document signed by Judge Rushton granting him a pardon.

The whole farce of his trial had merely been Richter's way of getting rid of someone who'd become a nuisance, he knew. And what better way to get rid of that nuisance right now than by putting him astride a sound horse and turning him loose – with Holly Platte and his bunch about to descend.

Richter must have decided that a weakened Bodie couldn't survive long with that gang after him. That it would be odds-on they'd run him down and kill him – and good damned riddance!

Bodie accepted his release with poker-faced calm, buckled on his gunbelt, fitted hat to head and sardonically thanked the sheriff for his release before quitting the jailhouse, a free man beneath a dark shadow.

So far so good, mused Sadler. And so it would seem. But not for long. Almost immediately things began to come apart, when instead of throwing his leg across his sturdy sorrel, Bodie looped the horse's lines over one arm and walked off, making for the livery.

124

'Bodie!' Sadler shouted after him. 'What the hell are you doin'?'

'Maybe saving your neck, badgepacker!' the reply drifted back.

Sadler didn't understand and Bodie had no time to explain. The prime factor for him here was that he knew the Plattes. And right now that pack was heading for here, hot on his trail. But the way he figured, knowing them as he did, once they discovered he'd been imprisoned and then freed again, they would go loco. Likely maybe even start in shooting up the place first and asking questions afterwards – if they ran true to form!

Who could tell with that breed? Maybe they'd punish the whole town for releasing the man they wanted dead. But a free Clay Bodie would never see that happen to *her* town, here . . . a town that might even one day get to be also his. . . .

CHAPTER 9

AND THE GUNS
MUST ROAR

The peaks of the Snow Wolf Mountains glowed dull red in the setting sun until it seemed as if the whole valley was encircled by the rim of a vast volcano.

The first stars were showing in a darkening sky as the sun went down and from the hills came the sounds of coyotes, welcoming the night.

Young Huck Platte was feeling full of iron decision as he stared into the flames of their supper fire close by the river. He'd felt confidence rising in him with every mile that brought them nearer to Big Bend. Gazing about him now he studied three of the most dangerous men in the Burning Hills whom he'd hired to back his play.

Why wire Holly to tell him they'd found Aaron's killer, he'd asked himself earlier? Why not ride back to Tolliver with the gunfighter's scalp hanging from his shell-belt instead? If four of them couldn't deal with just one man they were in the wrong line of business.

So it was decided.

Dour Conway Burns had smiled for the first time in days when youthful Huck announced his intention to go straight after Bodie the moment they hit Big Bend. A slender young man with hips so narrow they seemed scarcely wide enough to support the heavy double gunrig he wore, Burns was as keen as Huck to prove himself against a gunpacker with a rep like Bodie.

Though less eager than Burns, Tom Morgan still figured the plan had merit after he'd come to know there would be no changing Huck's mind anyway. The leathery outlaw reached that decision after realizing that should anything befall the kid in Big Bend, Holly would likely cut his heart out. Better to take his chances against Bodie with all the odds his way than find himself having to face Holly if things went wrong.

Barney Platte proved less enthusiastic about the proposal. Firstly, as he saw it, was the fact that Holly had given specific orders on what was to be done should their quarry be located and, secondly, because he had actually witnessed Clay Bodie gun down his lightning-fast kid brother. Right now Barney Platte reckoned Bodie to be the fastest man in Colorado Territory with the Colts – with the exception of brother Holly, of course.

But Holly was far away and if it was to be a choice between heading in after Bodie with three good men to back his play, or clashing with Huck, then backshooting Barney would choose going along with the kid every time.

'Knew I could count on you, Barney,' Huck grinned as they swung up and headed southwards along the starlit trail. After a time, Barney saw his brother take out his skinning knife and begin honing the blade to a razor's edge on his leather shotgun chaps. Barney didn't have to be told what this meant. When Huck threatened to lift Bodie's scalp, he'd meant it literally.

Within his mansion, secure behind sturdy walls and protected by his loyal henchmen, the general stood by the window of his War Room and gazed soberly down upon the flickering lights of Big Bend.

As always, Richter was clean-shaven and immaculately attired, with silvering hair brushed back and a distinct element of the military in the precise, perfect cut of his clothes.

The region's wealthiest man showed no outward emotion when gravel-voiced Reb Quent arrived with the latest news from town, yet underneath his right eye a small nerve began to pulse.

Bodie had not quit town!

Richter clasped his hands behind his back and rocked to and fro on polished boot-heels. The gun-fighter whose arrival in Big Bend had originally seemed to him like a fat plum dropped into his lap, had instead managed somehow to shake the very foundations of the secure world the big man had built around himself.

Bodie had forced him to take extreme measures in attempts to get rid of him. Yet now fate had twisted events in such a way that he'd been forced to set the troublemaker free in order to save the town – with the intention of putting paid to Bodie after this was done.

He quit rocking, unclasped his hands and forced himself to think more positively. Four outlaws against one wounded gunslinger. Surely the logical outcome could only be Clay Bodie in a pine coffin and Judah Richter stronger and more secure than ever in his fortress?

Turning, he stared out over the starlit rangelands at those remote mountain peaks of purest white rearing majestically in the distance, seemingly unsupported by the land in the deep night sky. The Snow Wolf Mountains were very much part of the land and continued to conceal their secrets well, but he knew he was on the verge of unlocking them now.

He nodded emphatically.

He would shortly force the Snow Wolfs to yield up their treasures . . . just as he would have that dark-haired beauty surrender her love. One need and desire was as powerful as the other and he would claim both yet . . . for he'd never been a man who could lose.

Richter stirred at a sound. Standing by his side Quent gestured northwards. Out on the starlit trail the dark shapes of horsemen were to be seen closing swiftly upon the silent town.

Bodie stood in the shadows before the Tambourine Saloon as the slow thudding of hoofbeats rose from the direction of the main trail.

His breathing was deep and even. All about him Big Bend lay unnaturally still and dark. No music drifted from the saloons and Abraham Street lay empty and lifeless before him but for a solitary hound dog which slunk by with shoulders trembling as though it was also aware of the strange tensions of the night.

The whisper had escaped that there were killers on the trail and the good folk of Big Bend had prudently retreated behind locked doors and shuttered windows.

Horsemen at last appeared at the head of the street and Bodie drew his .45.

There was no reluctance in him tonight as there

had been when facing Blayney West and Rooney Van. They were amateurs he'd known he could deal with at will. But these nightriders were true *pistoleros,* the killer breed who asked for and gave no quarter.

He identified the powerful, wide-shouldered silhouette of young Huck Platte as that rider signalled with his left hand and led his henchmen down the block at a shuffling walk-trot. As they passed beneath a street lamp he saw light glinting on gunmetal in every hand.

His shoulders flexed and rolled smoothly within his leather vest as the horsemen drew closer. Even at a distance he could feel the danger radiating off them. Barney Platte appeared even larger and more menacing than the day he'd stood watching his kid brother spill his young life into the dust of Toryville, helpless with lawmen's gun covering him.

That had been a fair fight and Aaron Platte had died. But now came revenge. Bodie eased himself out of the shadows. 'Plattes! You should have stayed in the Burning Hills!'

They froze instantly in the shifting yellow light. There was a jarring sense of shock, a momentary weakening of resolve when they saw the man they were hunting reveal himself so confidently as though he were the hunter.

Then a hound whimpered beneath the store porch, and as though it were a signal the Burning Hills killers exploded into action and swung their

131

guns towards Clay Bodie.

Bodie's Colt thundered and his first bullet slammed Conway Burns out of his saddle to smash through the hotel hitchrail and go crashing down into the shadows, dead before his lips could touch the earth.

Hard on the heels of the first blast Bodie's second bullet took Barney Platte in the guts and he slumped across the neck of his mount and raked feebly with spur to go galloping away, reeling drunkenly in the saddle.

Huck Platte came galloping headlong for Bodie's alleymouth with gun belching flame while Tom Morgan hollered at the top of his lungs and sent hot lead howling across the street.

All bullets failed to find their target as Bodie had dived headlong when Barney Platte thundered by in a great whirl of dust. A diving leap carried him over the low fence in back of the hardware store. He bounced up to plunge headlong through a gap in the palings and reappeared on the street fifty feet away in a handful of seconds.

Huck Platte and Morgan sawed their horses back viciously and began blasting at shadows in the thick gloom of the alley. Bodie's six-gun crashed with fierce authority and Morgan lurched in the saddle yet somehow recovered to send red tracers of death whipping back.

Dropping belly-flat in deep dust, Bodie grimaced

and swung a smoking gunbarrel as Huck Platte came charging headlong, riding hands and heels and howling like a redskin. Flames belched from Bodie's hot .45 and Platte's racing mount went down on its jaws, hurling the rider high.

Morgan's fire howled close forcing Bodie to hurl himself desperately for the nearest cover while fingering fresh shells into his piece.

Suddenly hoofbeats thundered close.

Bodie dived headlong and rolled three times while still reloading his piece. Spinning with desperate speed he confronted the looming bulk of a horse and rider storming in from another direction, instinctively bobbed low beneath the wicked flare of Morgan's Big Sixer.

Resting on one shoulder, clutching his piece two-handed, he triggered, then triggered again, to bring down racing horse and rider in a billowing spume of dust with Morgan's death howl jagging down his spinal column like the bite of a bonesaw.

Next split-second, Bodie was struck.

The bullet ripped through his thigh muscle and knocked him off balance, but in doing so saving him from Platte's next bullet. Teeth locked, tears filling his eyes, Bodie fanned gun-hammer and emptied his cutter in a continuous rolling roar, his fire homing in on the bursting flares of Huck Platte's big black Colt. The killer's shadowy shape arched backwards with a jagged scream, and by the time Bodie's hammer finally clicked on empty he knew the man was dead.

Bodie rolled sluggishly yet somehow kicked to his feet.

He found he could walk – that bullet had not found bone as he'd feared.

As shifting veils of dust began to clear he dimly made out Morgan's motionless silhouette, then caught the gleam of sightless eyes. Some thirty feet farther on at the bullet-gouged south corner of the hardware store, Huck Platte lay on his broad back with weeping bullet-holes in his chest.

All that was to be seen of Conway Burns were his motionless big boots with worn holes in the soles protruding from the shadows of the hotel porch.

Dust and gunsmoke rose in a fog against the stars and somewhere in the distance drumming hoofbeats slowly faded.

Bodie limped towards the livery with deep creases furrowing lean cheeks. It was done. The Platte outlaws had failed in their mission but in doing so had succeeded in convincing him that neither this nor any other town could ever be home to a man like himself.

By this time tomorrow he would be across the border into New Mexico and back on the drift again ... the eternal Bodie drift stretching into forever now. . . .

Next instant he went diving low with his gun once again swinging towards the stutter of running feet.

134

He was within a breath of opening up when he glimpsed the flowing dark tresses, the billow of a flowered dress. With a groan of relief he came up out of the crouch and managed a haggard smile as she called his name.

'Oh, Clay . . . are you all right? Tell me you are. . . .'

He grimaced, feeling the strength draining from his body. He tried to speak but it sounded to his own ears as more like a snarl, as if he was still in killing mode.

The girl's steps slowed as she drew closer. She extended both hands like a person approaching a dangerous dog which nevertheless plainly needed help. It was only when her hands finally reached out to claim his that he shuddered and felt the iron tensions draining from him, leaving him weak.

'You're hurt, Clay,' she said, linking her arm through his. 'Come on, you're coming home with me now.'

He resisted, but weakly.

Tomorrow, he promised himself as he allowed himself to be led away from the street of death. He would definintely ride out tomorrow.

It was so long since Judah Richter had sipped from the bitter cup of defeat that the reality of it now left him slightly dazed and disbelieving. Even more unusual for the general on that bitter day after, was that he actually seemed resigned to listen to the advice and opinions of others.

'Look, you've already tried both the clever way and the quiet way, General,' he was told late the following afternoon with the town still in a state of shock. 'And it's all come to nothin'. The widow will never marry you now. You tried to force her hand because of that damned gunfighter but all it did was set her against you. . . .'

Quent's voice trailed off when he saw that the other's glass was now empty. The bodyguard grunted at Zachary Clint who silently took the glass, refilled it from the decanter in the mansion's front room, then returned to Richter who accepted it in brooding silence.

Beyond the mansion the day was unnaturally quiet. The town below was also stunned by the murderous ferocity of the shoot-out, most believing they were now waiting for Richter to tell them what their response should be to what could only be interpreted as a crushing defeat.

But today Quent had had enough of tension and uncertainty and was at last speaking his mind.

'Look, boss, you wanted that gold for your empire and for the woman so as to "set the final seal on your respectability" – these are your own words I'm quotin'. You figured you could see how you might have used one thing to get the other. But things went sour. Bodie did us a good turn when he got rid of

136

West for us, but then the dame crossed us all and turned to him.'

He paused to make a cutting gesture with his gun hand.

'You gotta forget the widow woman, boss man. She's slipped through your fingers. Gone . . . finished . . . goodbye blue-eyes! You gotta listen to me now.'

Richter gulped at his drink. What had just been said sounded ugly, and yet he knew it was nothing but the truth. Only that very morning Richter had visited Carrie to issue a final ultimatum regarding that gunfighter, yet the couple had been openly visible upon Main directly after his threat was delivered.

Once more he'd been defied. She would not discuss the gunfighter with him and refused to stop keeping company with the man. Yet was his gun-hand now hinting at a safer alternative?

'Go on,' the general growled.

Quent nodded briskly. 'A woman is just a woman, Mr Richter, but the Old German Mine is somethin' you can't afford to lose out on. You've told me that often enough, so now I'm remindin' you. Sure, you tried to wrap it up, and you tried damn hard. But the fact that it didn't work out don't mean the game's lost. How come, you might ask? On account you can still get that map, is how.'

'You tell me how, gunman.'

137

'Take it. Yeah, you heard. If you can't get it one way, get it any way you can. You know I'm right.'

For a moment the general appeared genuinely shocked. Until recently his wheelings and dealings in Big Bend might have occasionally been suspect and shady, but in the main he'd managed to maintain at least a veneer of fair dealing and honest practice. It was not until the coming of Bodie that he'd found himself forced to manipulate the law which he'd hitherto largely supported. He'd taken risks already but the fear of exposure had prevented his going too far. He greatly valued his reputation and was loath to risk it further.

Unless, of course, it could be done without risk as Quent was hinting.

His man's fixed stare never left him in that long minute. Hardcase Quent had been the general's right hand man and troubleshooter over several years, and both had profited from that union. He needed Quent's input desperately, and the man instantly sensed this.

'Listen, General, this whole damned town is on edge right now and it's not just Bodie that's raisin' the dust. The whole place has had the jitters ever since them killers showed the other night. Bodie knows there's at least some risk the rest of the Platte bunch might show any time, and it could be that's why he's holdin' out . . . him bein' such a gold-plated hero and all . . . just in case Holly Platte does show.'

He paused for effect, then went on more slowly and deliberately.

'Tell me, boss man, who would this here town blame if there *was* a robbery?'

Richter raised his gaze with a slow animation crossing his face as he realized what the other was hinting at. 'By Judas . . . him!' he breathed emotionally. But he instantly sobered as another thought came hard on the heels of the first. 'But . . . just a moment. Just say we got hold of that map, like you say, how could we afford to get away from town afterwards to go after the treasure without everyone getting suspicious?'

Eagerly and confidently Reb Quent told him, and slowly the general's smile returned but did not fade this time.

CHAPTER 10

A LEGEND DIES

Manny Martin was drunk as a brewer's cat, which meant he was a man totally at peace with his world.

The day had begun auspiciously for Manny with a couple of free early shots, courtesy of his new 'friend', Bodie, then had progressed in a pleasant and whiskey-tinted blur throughout the rest of the day. Until a cloudy midnight found Manny propping up the rear fence of an alley by the bank and singing, his sole company a scraggy black cat which was beginning to irk him by scratching at the palings.

Big Bend's lush drained his bottle, concentrated his aim upon the feline, then let fly. In his condition his aim could only be lousy. The bottle missed its target by fifteen feet and came within inches of shattering the rear window of the store next door. Yet his actions had the desired effect when the cat fled, leaving Manny alone again and free to pursue his muse. He sang:

> Oh, bury me lonesome,
>   Bury me deep,
> Bury me in a nightshirt,
>   So a man can get some sleep!

He fell silent when he heard that strange scratching sound again. Puzzled weaving, he surveyed his shadowy surrounds. Not a scratching cat or rodent to be sighted. Nothing in truth to be seen but the blank rear walls of the store and bank.

He considered the puzzling situation for a time until eventually it struck him. Of course! The scratching sound was coming from within the bank!

Puzzled and curious, he lurched the length of the bank's rear wall and rounded the corner to reach the heavy, steel-barred side door. The drunk knew every back alley and rear door in town and knew damn well this was *never* left open. Yet it was partially ajar right now as he confirmed that the insistent scraping sound he'd heard was coming from *inside*.

Too drunk to be either nervous or scared, Manny clumsily jerked the door fully open to be confronted by the spectacle of a bound and gagged figure sprawled upon the floor just inside. The banker was feebly scraping his thonged feet against the wall to create the sound that had attracted his attention.

All thumbs and panting heavily, it took Manny an unconscionably long time to get the gag out of an hysterical Roland Burney's jaws to hear him croak, '*The bank's been robbed!*'

Bodie was at the livery saddling his horse next morning when he glimpsed Carrie West walking across Abraham Street. Putting the finishing touches to the harness, he looped the reins over one arm and moved out into the sunshine to greet her.

'Morning, Carrie.'

She failed to return his smile. 'Is it true, Clay?' she demanded.

'About the bank? Yeah, I just heard. I'm fixing to go scout around some and see if I can pick up the bandits' sign.'

'That's the reason I came looking for you,' she panted. 'I believe I know who robbed the bank, and why. I even suspect I might also know where they've gone.'

'Are you serious?'

She was, as she had already revealed by the time they were seated in the sunny front window of the next-door diner a short time later. Carrie did not believe the robbery had been staged by outlaws, she insisted, nor did she believe they had been after money. Instead she felt all but certain it was the map left by her husband they had been looking for – his map of the vital Three Pines section of the Snow Wolf Mountains. In addition, she also now firmly believed she knew who'd both robbed the bank and stolen the map.

'The hell you say, girl!' he breathed. 'But . . . who?'

'The general!'

He blinked incredulously and she reached out to touch his hand.

'As you know already, the general rode out yesterday with Quent and the men, declaring he was going scouting for the Plattes. That was a lie, I'm certain. I believe they came back to town during the night, robbed the bank, and are now most likely on their way to the Snow Wolves.'

'But you told me you believed that map to be worthless.'

'That was before yesterday when Manny told me about Lucy Doolin. Of course I'd heard the rumours but never believed them. But that girl was real, nothing surer, and they got rid of her by sending her away.'

He was still shaking his head in puzzlement as she continued.

'I honestly believed Blayney loved me, Clay, it was all I had to cling to. But if he lied about one thing then it's very possible he lied about another. If he had struck it rich in the high country and kept it

143

from me, then it proves almost certainly he must have intended to run off with that girl, as the rumours had it. I must find out for sure, Clay, one way or the other. I must know the truth.'

'But how—?'

'You could take me up there. If the general is guilty as we suspect, and is also making for the Three Pines, then we should be able to pick up his trail without too much trouble.'

'But I can't quit Big Bend. If the Plattes show up—'

'We must know the truth, Clay. *I must!*'

Bodie's resistance began to falter. How could he deny her? And how could he turn his back on the possibility that evidence might prove that her husband had never loved her? For if that man's memory was no longer sacred in her eyes, might it not be possible that Carrie might one day begin to see himself – Clay Bodie – as a real flesh and blood man, not just some stranger of the gun she had come to for help?

It was crazy and likely dangerous. But he knew he would do it. He had no choice . . . now.

Up here at the six thousand feet level the thin air cut like an Apache scalp axe. But neither cold, exhaustion nor the rugged terrain daunted General Richter as he rested upon a lichened boulder, running gold dust through his fingers and breathing heavily.

'The Lost German!' he said reverently. 'So it *was* true!'

144

A rare smile worked Reb Quent's cold-chapped features. It was Quent who'd first trailed Blayney West up into the Snow Wolves a month earlier upon hearing a whisper of a major strike. West had proven far too crafty and trail-wise to lead him to his mine, but the prospector's elaborate precautions to shake him off had convinced both Quent and subsequently Richter that there had to be substance behind the rumours.

So Richter had immediately approached West with an offer to buy in, this despite the fact that the two men were anything but friendly due entirely to the general's lustful interest in the other man's wife. But West had denied all knowledge of any strike, yet continued to lavish expensive gifts upon his red-lipped tart from Tolliver.

The general had initially avoided West up to the day his accountant presented the annual review of his current financial status. The document revealed that Richter had all but emptied his coffers in maintaining both his lofty position in town and his big spread, so that with his campaign for the senate coming up the next year he now needed big money, and fast.

From that very moment Blayney West's fate had been sealed.

There was in existence a map of the site which West had let be known was in the safe keeping of his

attorney. This was done in order that everyone would
know that, should anything befall him, the map
would pass directly on to his wife and their hard-
nosed attorney who could be entrusted with its
ongoing protection.

This didn't bother the rich man, for ambitious
Judah Richter had always planned to wed the widow
– just as soon as her husband was safely in the
ground.

But this still left the problem of exactly how West
might best be eliminated. Due to his prominence in
the town the general could not simply dispatch
Quent to deal with the prospector. He must bide his
time until an opportunity presented itself, and he
believed that time had come the day the drummer
rode into town to report encountering Clay Bodie
heading in.

Quent had immediately launched into action and
summoned West to the mansion to convince the gunslinger that Bodie had caused the death of his sister.

Blayney West's notorious temper had exploded. So
he challenged Brodie and been shot down, yet
Quent's respect for Bodie's gunspeed held him back
until what was to happen next.

The general had decreed that Bodie must die,
after which it would simply be a matter of time,
patience and careful planning for Richter to court
and wed the widow, get his hands on that map and at
long last achieve all his dreams.

But it did not quite work out that way when Clay Bodie proved impossible either to catch or kill. This forced the general to reconsider and make alternative plans, which had eventually seen him succeed with his bogus trial of the gunfighter until eventually forced to have Bodie released when grave danger threatened.

But that was now all in the past. Every mistake and regret was blanketed out by the shimmering promise of yellow gold, and Richter was actually smiling to himself – a rare spectacle – when a single pebble clattered down from above the rocky wall they were carefully negotiating.

Every eye snapped upwards. At first there was nothing to be seen above but boulders and pines and the scattered snowdrifts which had been the guardians of the German's mine for so long. But then came the tiny trickle of pebbles which had followed the first falling stone, and which quickly swelled into a clattering stream.

Richter bawled an order and they rushed for their mounts, while two hundred feet above, Clay Bodie and Carrie West were mounting weary horses.

'Oh, Clay, I'm sorry,' gasped the girl. 'It's just that when I realized it was all true, when what we discovered proved that my husband had struck it rich . . . I just stepped back and dislodged that rock and—'

'It's all right,' Bodie insisted, staring downwards, and prayed he might be proved right. It was a long

147

way back to Big Bend and even should they make it, there could be no guarantee they would be capable of convincing the town of the general's obvious guilt. Yet they would have to try. It was their only chance.

Mayor Roland Burney flinched at the sound of a shot and scuttled to the bank window to peer out.

Directly across the street a man with the face of a ferret was grinning as he blew smoke from his gun barrel. The outlaw then twirled the six-gun on his forefinger and slouched off down Abraham Street to pass beneath the bullet-holed advertising sign he'd just finished shooting up.

In the absence of law and order this town seemed to be coming apart fast.

The mayor swabbed at his forehead as he turned to face his fellow citizens. There were a dozen men in the bank, representing the leading citizens of Big Bend.

Just a few hours earlier these citizens along with others, had been reluctantly assisting the general in his fruitless search for Carrie West and Clay Bodie. The searchers had been reluctant volunteers for despite the fact that Bodie was a gunslinger, the man had won widespread support in Big Bend, particularly since the trumped-up trial. And Carrie West was still, as Manny Martin would have put it, 'The finest lady in this man's town . . . by a mile.'

148

Yet despite their reluctance to go along with the story of the Lost German Mine which Bodie and Carrie had brought back from the Snow Wolfs overnight, Big Bend had still done as the general had bid. For Richter was still their figurehead and benefactor, was still the paternal master of Big Bend, so if the general claimed that Carrie West and Clay Bodie had conspired to murder Blayney West, then surely it must be so?

But that was before the killers came.

Six abreast, they'd come riding down Abraham Street, and there was not a boy over sixteen years of age who didn't recognize the fierce, craggy features of Holly Platte with wounded brother Barney riding by his side.

There followed a period of explosive confrontation with the Bodie-hunting towners on one side facing the Bodie-hunting killers from the north.

Had a single shot exploded during those electric minutes of confrontation, bloodshed would have been inevitable. But nobody had touched off that first shot, mainly due to the fact that General Richter had swiftly realized that he and Holly Platte shared a common cause.

A man was at large somewhere in Big Bend, a man they both wanted dead. What could be more inevitable than that they should join forces to hunt him down?

With two dead brothers clamouring for vengeance from their graves, and reluctant to lose anybody else

149

in this dangerous hick town, Holly Platte readily agreed to join forces, and there was no time wasted with the leaders agreeing to shake hands on their common cause before resuming the hunt.

It was the spectacle of General Richter actually shaking hands with Holly Platte that had sickened Mayor Burney and caused him to quit the manhunt immediately.

The mayor had no more courage than the next citizen, yet had somehow found what it took to stand up to Quent when that man threatened him should he back out. With more dignity and resolve than the town had seen from him in a long time, Burney had walked back to his bank and from that vantage point onwards flatly refused all threats and blandishments to align himself with a pack of killers regardless of the consequences.

The banker's action set an example which every man in Big Bend still worthy of that name, found impossible to ignore.

Jud Dalton and Clancy Ekron were the first to follow Burney back to the bank, followed shortly afterwards by hotel-keeper Phil Forgen, blacksmith Buck Garrett and Haines Hall of the stage depot. Soon there there were upwards of a score of grim yet determined citizens congregated behind the bank's closed doors, when that sharp knock sounded.

'Don't open it, Roland,' Hall said nervously. 'Could be one of them bloody-handed outlaws.'

'Or then again, it might be the general,' suggested Ekron.

It proved to be neither, and when postmaster Bob Toomey identified himself he was admitted without hesitation.

Toomey was scared, just like them, and sweated, also as they did. But he was the only man in town with a crisp yellow telegraph slip clutched in his fist.

'You're not gonna believe this boys,' the man grinned, 'but this here is for Mr Bodie . . . and it just come in from Captain Frank Chase in Denver!'

'Forget it then,' Burney growled, fingering the drapes to peer out nervously. 'He'll never live to read it.'

'Well, you fellers are gonna hear it anyway – and right now,' Toomey countered, and, clearing his throat, began to read:

Response to your request on information concerning one Judah Richter stop Former Union sergeant not general who deserted army in 1862 and joined Quantrill's Raiders stop Profiteered in Mexico post war and is wanted for murder there stop

Toomey lowered the slip and looked up. 'It's from Captain Chase, It was sent on the Denver telegraph.'

'Quantrill!' breathed Dalton, who'd lost family members during the Quantrill raid on Blackstone,

Kansas. His face was ashen, 'The general rode with bloody Quantrill!'

There was a stunned silence as honest men digested the grottesque truth that Judah Richter was not the war hero they'd respected, but far worse than being a mere imposter, had ridden with Quantrill, the most hated man in the United States.

And at that very moment, outside this bank in their town, this murderous imposter was hunting down a man and woman in the company of scum of his own kind!

It was Dalton who first took out his revolver. More weapons instantly appeared. Something raw and unquenchable was rising from the very boards, and suddenly, empoweringly, they were feeling and acting like real men again as the mayor flung open the doors and led them out into the street.

Bodie returned to the chink in the cellar door to peer out and see the Richter bunch drawing closer to this abandoned house where they'd taken shelter.

Bodie told himself that Zachary Clint and Buck Wheeler were dead men. There was no way he could miss at this range when the searchers opened the doors. But Richter, Holly Platte and others were less than a half block away. The shooting would bring them running, and he would surely die.

She must die, also. And turning to look at her, he knew beyond any doubt that they would have been destined to share a future together – had they lived.

He reached for her hand in silence and squeezed tightly . . . until suddenly the searchers were so close Bodie could hear their muttered voices. In moments they would be at the door. . . .

He was stepping back to have a full range of fire when shooting erupted and he heard startled yells outside. Pressing his eye to a chink he glimpsed running figures then saw a man fall in Abraham Street when a heavy rifle thundered deafeningly.

What the hell was happening?

It didn't take long to find out when they realized the fallen man was Barney Platte. Moments later two men moved into their vision, blasting with rifles.

It was Mayor Burney and storekeeper Dalton!

What in hell was happening?

Before that question found an answer, a swarm of towners came running into the street, toting weapons.

That did it!

In seconds he was out that door with a .45 in his fist and Carrie's desperate cry in his ears. He didn't turn back, could not. Dragging his leg a little, he sighted Wheeler a short distance ahead behind the partial cover of a fence, shooting at somebody to his right. He propped, triggered – and Wheeler crashed face downwards with his blood soaking the grass.

The whole street was immediately a battleground.

153

Bodie sprinted across the side street to sight gun flashes flaring from the Red Light Saloon with two hard-faced citizens closing in on the building . . . and another dead man sprawled in the dust.

His heart leapt as he realized more towners were appearing, some armed with weapons, some toting hay forks and clubs, but all converging on the one target – the Red Light where gunsmoke belched from windows and doors.

He kept running and others were joining him. He couldn't tell who they were through the gunsmoke but knew they were men just like himself, fighting because they knew they must, ready to die if that was what it took to free this town from those who would take it from them.

The towners reached the saloon behind a thunder of guns, the howls of pain . . . the spectacle of some hellion running from a side door of the building with his clothing aflame.

Bodie was first in through the doors, his bucking Colt spewing flame and death at close quarters as men fought back, ran, or died. Two slugs slammed though Holly Platte's snarling mouth and his tumbling corpse crashed against Reb Quent and knocked him into Mayor Burney's line of fire. Above the thunder of battle then – the general's booming voice, hysterical, disbelieving, refusing to comprehend it all could have all gone so wrong, so swiftly.

It seemed every towner's weapon homed in on that voice, and Judah Richter fell, plunging into an eternity prepared – not for 'the Devil and his Angels' as prophesied in the Bible – but rather into that final terrifying place of judgement reserved exclusively for all those who'd once ridden with Quantrill.

And then the battle was over and Big Bend was finally free . . . and, once again, poor.

The first crisp bite of an early fall was in the air that day a month later when the stranger rode into Big Bend astride a skewbald mare. They didn't know his name but recognized his breed. Two low-slung guns, frozen eyes, the very arrogance of his carriage announced that this was yet another of the breed which they had unwillingly learned to know on sight.

Gunslinger.

This one didn't waste words. He'd heard famed Clay Bodie was living here and wanted to see him. Like, pronto.

Manny Martin first gave him the sad news, then took the fast gun out to Boot Hill where he was shown the new grave with the handsome marker bearing the inscription:

CLAY BODIE
1860–1890
R.I.P

Denver Clint Smith was bitterly disappointed. Sure, he'd heard Bodie had been killed here in remote Big Bend, but had to come see for himself. He was a glum figure as he took a drink with the locals at the Tambourine and, after hearing the full account of the great gun battle, morosely filled leather and rode off in search of some other famous name to add to his list of kills.

As the killer quit town, drinkers emerged on the saloon porch to watch him go. Without his moustache, with flowing locks now trimmed short, and most of all, without a gun on his hip, Clay Bodie looked little different from any other townsman.

Of course there would always be the risk that someone in Big Bend might spill his secret, Bodie was aware as he selected and lighted a fat cigar, yet he reckoned the chances slim. For about him sprawled a township at least as prosperous as it had been in the heyday of the general's patronage. The general was dead and gone, but 'Mr Walker the gunsmith' had stepped into his shoes.

Clay Bodie reckoned there was enough gold up in the Lost German Mine to sustain Big Bend for a lifetime . . . a lifetime's peace. . . .

He stepped down into the street of the town.

His town.

He inhaled deeply and began walking east towards Lee Street. In an empty grave at Big Bend's Boot Hill, the legend of Clay Bodie, gunfighter, lay buried. Yet

Bodie the man survived, and that man had never felt more intensely alive than now when, turning the corner, he saw Carrie waiting for him at the gate . . . as she would do for the rest of their lives. Together.

28 4 25